What He Don't Know Won't Hurt:

A Lustful Love Triangle

A Novel

BY: NIKALOS

Copyright © 2019 Solakin Publication

This is a work of fiction. Names, characters, places, and incidents are wither the product of the author's imagination or are used fictitiously, and any resemblance to actual persons, living or dead, business establishments, events, or locales, is entirely coincidental.

DEDICATION

THIS BOOK IS DEDICATED TO THE WORD
LOVE. LOVE IS LIKE A POWERFUL DRUG AND
SHOULDN'T BE MISUSED.

PROLOGUE

SASHA

This was the happiest day of my life. I had been dreaming about this day since I was a little girl. I was only twenty-two years old, and already my fairytale was coming true; I was about to marry the man of my dreams. Sometimes I couldn't help but to sit and think about all the bullshit I had been through in life, but I was grateful to have made it through my hardships. Even though I had a horrible childhood, I still felt that, at the end of the day, I was blessed. So many people went throughout life spending it alone, never finding the right person that would give them that unconditional love. The love that a woman craves from her significant other is a love that everyone on Earth isn't always blessed to have. I was one of the lucky women who was actually getting the chance to marry my soulmate, and I had already made my vow to the man above that I would never forsake him.

Us marrying wasn't because I was pregnant like most people were thinking, but it was honestly because we loved one another. We wanted to make it official, and we wanted the world to know that we were one mind, body, and soul.

"Are you sure you're ready to do this?" Sweet Pea whispered in my ear as she brushed my Brazilian weave and pulled it in a high bun on top of my head.

"I know you may think I'm crazy for settling down, but I love him. This is the man I want to spend the rest of my life with."

Sweet Pea made an odd face before mumbling, "I just don't see how you can walk away from all this college dick you could possibly be getting, to settle down with Ryan."

I rolled my eyes and began to apply a little makeup to my caramel skin complexion.

Sweet Pea and I had been best friends since elementary school, and we always kept it real with one another. Growing up in school, Sweet Pea had a hard time getting a boyfriend. She didn't start dating until high school because niggas always had something smart to say about her weight. Sweet Pea had a baby face that made her look innocent, but she was far from that. She was medium in height, with milky brown complexion, and was considered a BBW.

I knew deep down in her heart that the only reason why Sweet Pea didn't want me to marry Ryan was because she had never found her true love, and she probably felt the shit didn't exist. I also felt she didn't want me to forget about our friendship, but there was no way in hell I could ever forget about my bestie.

Our eyes connected in the mirror and we smiled at one another.

"At the end of the day, Sasha, if you happy with getting married and throwing away your twenties, then I will be happy for you too."

I couldn't help but laugh at Sweet Pea's sarcasm.

"Will you do me a favor and help me get dressed instead of making jokes about me throwing away my freedom?"

Sweet Pea sighed.

"I guess I might help you walk to your doom. But I warned you, Sasha, marriage ain't what it's cracked up to be. Just think, we trading club hopping and drinking until we throw up, to changing poopy diapers Monday through Sunday," Sweet Pea taunted.

Sweet Pea and I both laughed before we finally became serious.

"I'm going to be serious for a minute; if you really want to do this, then you know I got your back."

"I know you do, Sweet Pea, now help me with my dress."

As I slid on my white wedding dress and shoes, I couldn't help but be amazed at how sexy I looked in the huge floor mirror.

A knock on the door signaled to me that the wedding was about to start.

"You look fine as hell for your special day," Sweet Pea confessed.

"Thank you."

Sweet Pea embraced me in a hug before she disappeared out the side door.

I took a deep breath to try to calm my nerves. I grabbed my silver necklace and said a small prayer. I headed out the door just when my younger brother Andre came to take my hand. I didn't have anyone to give me away so Andre took it upon himself to be the man who walked me down the aisle.

Even though Andre was now twenty years old, I still felt like the older sister who was responsible for protecting him. As I looked him up and down, I wasn't even going to lie, my brother was looking good in his all-white tuxedo. Andre was six feet, slim, brown skinned, and always rocked a low cut and kept a clean face. He always had some chick on his arm that was willing to do anything to please him. My brother just had that effect on certain women.

When he took my hand and the music began to play, my stomach began to feel as if it was doing somersaults.

"Don't worry, I got you," Andre whispered in my ear.

When I burst through the double doors, all eyes were on me, but I decided to not acknowledge anyone. All I cared about was getting my ass down the aisle so I could be with Ryan. Luther Vandross's "Here and Now" played softly in the background. Flashing lights flashed as I walked past some of my former teachers and Ryan's family.

As Luther Vandross played in the distance, tears began to fall down my face. I was ruining my makeup, but today was an emotional day. Today was about me and the man I was going to spend the rest of my life with. My heart was beating hard as hell and it felt as if it was about to jump into my lap.

As I continued down the aisle, I couldn't help but be amazed at how beautiful the church was decorated. The aisle was covered with purple rose petals, and the smell of the roses filled my nose. As I made my way to the altar, the man of my dreams was standing there waiting on me, looking sexier than ever.

Ryan was about six feet two, light skinned, and 178 pounds, with a crisp clean haircut with deep wavy hair. His tuxedo was all white with a purple stripe down the middle. My man was on point, and I didn't dare take my eyes off him as we said our vows and declared our love for one another. Once the wedding was over, I was glad to walk out of the First Monument Baptist Church. Ryan and I didn't hold back any affection for one another. As I stared into his eyes and as his lips met mine, my soul was finally at peace. I felt as if I was dreaming, and I was in disbelief that I had just married the love of my life. I smiled as the limo pulled up at the church stairs and didn't hesitate to hop my happy ass inside. We kissed and caressed each other's bodies the whole ride to the hotel. The tapping on the window was the only reason why we pulled away from each other.

"Sasha, I love you so much," Ryan said, opening the door to the limo.

I pulled him toward me and gave him a fat wet kiss on his soft lips.

"I love you more, baby," I whispered into his ear.

"Baby, you ain't never got to worry about nothing," he assured me as he grabbed my hand and helped me out the limo. When he told me those words, I felt it in my soul that he meant every word.

I was surprised when he turned me around and placed a blindfold over my eyes. I had never really been a big fan of surprises, but since it was my wedding day, I figured Ryan had planned something special. He held my hand tightly and helped steer me throughout the noisy hallway of the hotel. I could smell the aroma of coffee being made as I followed him to our destination. The elevator dinged in the distance, and a few moments later, the elevator doors closed behind us.

Ryan's lips met mine as he pushed me up against the elevator wall and began to rub his hands over my sensitive body. My clitoris was throbbing for his touch, and all I truly wanted to do at that moment was to remove the blindfold so I could see exactly what was going on. When the elevator dinged and we got off, we headed straight towards our room. The blindfold was finally removed, and I was amazed to see that the room had been decorated just for this special night. Ryan grabbed my hand as we walked through the dimly lit room. We passed the Jacuzzi and headed right for the king-sized bed that was covered with purple rose petals that made the letter S.

"Thank you, baby, for all of this. I love it," I revealed as I placed a gentle kiss on his lips.

"You know I aim to please," Ryan whispered in my ear.

He chuckled as he turned me around and unzipped the back of my dress. I stepped out of my long white dress as he grabbed me in an embrace. He didn't waste any time lying me down on the bed and devouring my mouth. His lips on mine had my mind straight gone, but that didn't stop me from trying to hurry and unsnap his shirt buttons as fast as I could. I hurried and undressed him as he began to place kisses on my neck and my chest. I could feel my juices flowing down my leg as he wrapped his lips around my mouth. When he pulled his nine-inch dick out of his boxers, I already knew it was about to go down. I licked my lips as my body began to crave for his touch. His dick poked me in my stomach as he laid on top of me and started back kissing and sucking on my hotspots.

"Sasha, thank you, baby, for marrying me. I love you so much. I have never loved a woman as much as I love you," he admitted as he stared into my soul.

He brushed my hair out of my face as he stared into my eyes.

"You will never have to worry about nothing," he promised me just before he placed a kiss on my forehead.

"Baby, I love you too, honey," I cried as I stared into his hazel eyes.

"Baby, let me read something to you," Ryan said before he slid off me and dug into his pants pockets.

My body ached for his touch, but I knew that Ryan wasn't going to keep me waiting for long. I watched him as he pulled a small piece of paper from his pants pocket and stood before me naked as he began to read from the paper.

"To my beautiful wife ... I promise to always put you first. I promise I will never leave your side. You are the only one I want in my life. I promise everything will be okay. You are my world, my everything, my best friend, soulmate, and now my wife. I love you more than life itself." As he continued to read the letter, tears began to fall down my face.

"Sasha, you have my heart for the rest of my life." He dropped the letter, and I pulled him towards me. Our tongues danced together as he caressed his hands up my thighs. He pulled away only to begin kissing the side of my neck where his name was tattooed. Right before my twenty-first birthday, we got our name tattooed on one another. I chose my neck, and he chose his chest. He always said he chose his chest because he wanted to keep me close to his heart.

I moaned as his hands began to roam up and down my body. I was dripping wet as he began to kiss and suck on each of my nipples until they were both hard as a rock. I eased my hand down towards his dick and began to stroke him with the palm of my hand as he groaned softly in my ear. He had me craving his nine-inch gorilla dick, and I wasn't going to be satisfied until he had me screaming and moaning his name. Just before he was about to slide into my wetness, I pushed him off me gently and headed over to the CD player and found the song that I was looking for. When Beyoncé's "Dance For You" started blasting, I went to the top of the bed and did the dance Ryan loved so much.

"Give it to me, baby. Bounce that ass," Ryan demanded as I grabbed the headboard and began to make my ass shake all in his face.

He was amazed at how I could make both my ass cheeks bounce, but what really threw him off was when I came down and hit a split. I flipped over on my back and spread my legs open as wide as I could to make sure to give him a view of what he had been missing all day. Ryan worked day in and day out, so we barely had time to be intimate like we wanted to. When we did find time, I always made sure my sex game was up to his standards. He wasn't a picky nigga, but he loved it when I kept my pussy hair trimmed to his liking. I always made sure to keep my pussy well-groomed like a pretty little garden.

Ryan smiled down at me as his fingers began to play with my pussy hairs. Just his touch sent chills up my spine. He held my hand and kissed the back of it just before he inserted his dick inside of me. I moaned as he slowly began to fill me up. I cried out as he gripped my thighs tightly and began to push in and out of my tight little pussy. He pulled out only to caress my clit with his tongue. My eyes rolled to the back of my head as I gripped the sheets as he pleased me with his mouth. I was in a sexual trance at that very moment, and there was no coming out of it any time soon. I grabbed the back of his head, forcing his tongue further inside me as he licked up my pussy juices. Ryan had a gift that none of my exes had yet to master; he knew how to fuck me, and he knew how to eat my pussy. When he pulled away from my pussy, he didn't stop there. He then began to lick his tongue up and down my thighs. Damn, that shit was giving me goosebumps all over my thighs as he hit all the right spots that turned me on.

He allowed his tongue to run up and down my legs until he came to my feet and placed my toe in his mouth.

"Mmm ... Yess..." I moaned out as I caressed my nipples.

When he slid his nine-inch cobra dick back inside me, I couldn't help but scream and moan his name. He slowly pushed himself in and out of my pussy as I tightened my pussy muscles. I was gyrating my hips and making sure to meet each thrust that he sent my way. Ryan placed my leg over his shoulder and kept thrusting in and out at a nice slow pace. The wetness between my legs dripped down my legs as he pushed deeper inside of me.

"Don't stop, daddy! You know I love this shit!" I screamed at the top of my lungs.

Ryan was drilling me like this was the first piece of ass he was getting fresh out of prison. He didn't let up, and his aggressiveness was only making my pussy become wetter than a lake. I bit down the inside of my lip as he began hitting my g-spot.

After about an hour of letting Ryan have his way with me, I pushed him on his back and straddled him. I stared into his sweaty face as I grinded my pussy on his nine-inch dick. I screamed as he held me tightly while he ripped my pussy walls into pieces.

I bounced up and down on his dick with heavy force, as sweat began to drip down my face. I leaned down and kissed him passionately as I began slow grinding on his dick. As our tongues wrestled in each other's mouths, the more my hips increased its speed. When our lips parted, I had a small surprise for him. I stuck my finger in my mouth as I slowly turned around without his dick slipping out of my tight pussy.

"Sss," Ryan moaned.

I knew my porn star spin was going to blow his mind. I continued rolling my hips as I yelled out his name. I was hornier than a motherfucker and wanted nothing more than to fuck all night. I held on to all my strength as I sat up with my back facing him. I bounced on the head of his dick as my juices dropped down my legs onto his stomach.

"Shit," he moaned as he slapped my ass cheeks.

I smiled as I looked back and watched as his dick slide in and out of me.

"Damn!" he yelled out as I began to ride him harder.

I smirked because I knew it was only a matter of time before he tapped out. I slid off of him and began attacking his dick with my tongue. I allowed my tongue ring to tease the tip of his head as I played with his balls. The taste of me filled my mouth as I began to deep throat his dick. He rubbed on my nipples as I slurped and sobbed on his manhood.

"Damn, ma ... Shit!" he cried out.

I increased my speed because I knew he was about to nut.

"Stop playing with me; give it to me now!" I demanded as I stroked him harder until that thick cream filled my mouth. I stared up at him as I swallowed every drop of him.

"Mmm," I moaned, wiping my mouth with the back of my hand.

His cum tasted so good; he had the best nut I had ever tasted. Most dudes, they shit be bitter as hell, but Ryan always drunk a lot of pineapple juice. I figured that's why his shit was so sweet. He pulled me toward him and kissed me softly on my lips. We were both exhausted and tired, and it wasn't long before Ryan had dozed off into a deep sleep. As I laid on his chest, I knew that I had made the right decision by marrying Ryan. He was the man of my dreams. He was the best thing that ever happened to me, and I promised to love him for all eternity.

SASHA

TEN YEARS LATER

The sun was shining bright and beautiful. The birds were chirping loudly, squirrels were running up and down the trees, and it seemed like everyone had something to do but me. I stared out my bedroom window thinking this was it for me. When people viewed my life, they tended to only look at the big expensive house, the cars, jewelry, and the name brand clothes that took up all of my closet space, but none of the material things meant shit to me. If people really took the time to study my inner self, I promise they would have known that I was a woman who was lonely and wanted some excitement in my life. I loved my family with all my heart and soul, but I did the same thing every single day, which was beginning to drive me crazy.

Every morning, I woke up at seven, cooked breakfast, got my children ready for school, and woke my husband up so he wouldn't be late for work. We all sat at the kitchen table, ate breakfast like a normal family, and when everyone was all done, they get up to go about their day, leaving me stuck in the house.

"Malcolm, get up!" I yelled, pulling the bed sheet from his head.

"Just let me sleep a little more," he groaned.

"Boy, if you don't get your butt up, I will drag you out this bed," I raved.

Malcolm was eight years old and took his daddy's height and light-skinned complexion. The only thing Malcolm had of mine was my thick eyebrows. He stayed in the mirror brushing his deep wavy hair, and swore up and down that he had all the girls in his class fighting over him. He was a huge basketball fan, and always said that one day he was going to play in the NBA. The coaches constantly bragged on how talented my son was and how far they thought he was going to go in life. This always would put a smile on face. I wanted the best for my son, and I always made sure that I stayed in his corner.

After Malcolm finally slid out of bed, I left out his room so he could get dress. I walked down the hallway and entered my seven-year-old's bedroom. Ashanti was snoring like a baby bear. I was still puzzled how a small child like my daughter could keep up so much fuss. Ashanti was my little princess and took her looks after me. She was caramel in complexion, and we looked as if we could have been twins. She was my mini me, and I loved her to the moon and back.

Ashanti's room was painted pink, with a princess pink bed, two drawers where she kept her clothes, and a 32-inch flat screen TV. I walked over to where her small radio was playing and turned it off, as I pulled the pink and white blanket from over her head. When I touched the bottom of her feet, she jumped up like a jack in the box and groaned when she noticed me standing over her. I could tell by her facial expression that she wasn't in the mood to get up and get ready for school. Ashanti already knew that her facial expression wasn't going to let her stay home from school.

Ashanti hated going to school and always was trying to come up with some excuse why she couldn't go. Malcolm was the complete opposite and loved going to school. I mean, he rarely missed any days. I laughed to myself because the only reason Malcolm loved school so much was because he liked playing basketball and being the class clown.

After I had managed to get Ashanti up and ready for school, I headed to my bedroom to wake my husband, who was lying on his back with his hand placed on his dick, while his other hand was hanging from the bed. I eased up on the bed next to him and slipped my hand under the bed sheets as I began to play with his sleeping dick. I gently began to massage him up and down until his dick began to become stiff. His hand grabbed mine and pulled me towards him. I gave him a kiss on the lips then playfully slapped him on his thigh.

"Breakfast ready, honey," I whispered in his ear.

"Give me a second," Ryan yarned.

Ryan and I had been married for only ten years, and he still was the best thing that ever happened to me. He came into my life at the worst time and showed me just what love truly meant. I still remembered how we met.

It was a Friday night. I had just gotten paid from my bullshit ass job and I was happy as hell to finally be free and decided to head out and have a little fun with my home girls. We all wanted to celebrate my freedom, so we decided to go out to the Sand Trap because it was ladies' night and everything was free.

I was rocking a pair of Gucci shades, a black, silk Gucci dress, tights, and six-inch Gucci heels. When I did step out the car that night, hoes wanted to kill me because their niggas couldn't take their eyes off me. To be honest, I wasn't even checking for no nigga, but that didn't stop the hoes from hating on me. Every time I walked, my ass jiggled, and niggas didn't hesitate to take a peek. As soon as we strolled through the front door, the DJ had that bitch to the ceiling. He had Khia's "Don't Trust No Nigga" blasting. I threw my hands up and began to rap the lyrics to the song. I sipped on my drink and didn't give a fuck about anybody. I danced my way to the center of the dance floor, grabbed some nigga I didn't know, and threw my ass on him. When I lifted up my head, the whole club stopped and made a circle around me. I mean all eyes were on me and I loved the shit. There was no way I was about to disappoint the crowd and let them down, so you already know I was turnt up. I placed my hands on my knees and started bouncing my ass against the nigga's body. I heard my home girls scream out my name in the distance, encouraging me to handle that business. I dropped to the floor then came back up really quick. That's when I went in extra hard and grabbed the front of his pants. I bent over as he walked up on me, and twerked my ass like a mad woman. His dick was poking me in my ass as he grabbed me and pushed up on me. When I turned around, our eyes connected. I swear shit begin to move in slow motion. I threw one of my legs up and began grinding over his body.

The way my performance was, I swear it could have been a soft porn flick because I was grinding the shit out of him. When the song ended, I was out of breath, and I needed something to drink. On my way to the bar, the nigga I was dancing with me stepped to me, and I immediately checked him out. I quickly estimated that his entire gear was less than three hundred dollars if that. He was rocking a number 23 Chicago Bulls Jersey, black denim, a pair of white Air Forces, and a gold chain. It was nothing that would usually get my attention, but I couldn't deny the fact that he was sexy as hell.

When he told me his name was Ryan and asked mine, I started to give him a fake name, but I decided against it. Instead, we exchanged numbers that night and started texting and talking on the regular.

When I found out that the only reason Ryan was at the club was because he was celebrating that he had just received a full scholarship to Albany State University, I was in shock because this nigga wasn't a dumb nigga.

While Ryan attended Albany State University, him and I dated for about two years before we both decided to get married. Ryan ended up landing a job as a paralegal after two years at Albany State University. I was there every step of the way as Ryan worked and slaved for his success. I was never the type of bitch to tell my man I didn't want kids until he made it big. These days shit wasn't guaranteed. There was no way I was going to wait until he had reached his goal before I started popping out babies. Two years into our marriage I started popping the kids out back to back. Ryan always said he wanted his family to be secure, and he worked his ass off so I could have anything my heart desired.

All he required me to do was take care of the house, sit around, and look cute. At first things were okay, but I had never been the type to be naïve, and I always wanted things for myself also.

If I had to describe myself in a nutshell, I would start by saying I was five feet even, 140 pounds, and thick in all the right places. I didn't have a lot of breasts, but I did have hips. I was caramel brown in complexion and kept my hair cut short. I had received a degree in business management from Troy University while I was pregnant with Ashanti. I wasn't a dumb bitch and didn't want to be the type of woman who depended solely on her husband only for him to divorce me twenty years later. I never wanted to be the one who didn't have a college degree and no job to provide for myself or my kids.

"Mom, the bus is about to come," Ashanti said, pulling my thoughts from the past and bringing me back to reality. After Ashanti kissed Ryan goodbye, she followed me out to the bus stop and waited for the bus to pull up. I waved at Malcolm's best friend mom as she pulled up in my driveway to pick Malcolm up for school.

After Ashanti was situated on the bus, I walked over to where Malcolm was standing waiting on me.

"Good morning, Sasha. I wanted to know if you wanted Malcolm to ride home with me after school."

"Hey, Tamara, and yes, that's fine. I don't mind."

I kissed Malcolm goodbye and waited until Tamara had pulled out my driveway before I headed back inside the house.

When I stepped back into the house, Ryan was standing in the middle of the kitchen talking on his phone. It had to have been a serious conversation because his forehead was wrinkled and he looked to be in deep thought. I didn't want to disturb him, so I decided to start cleaning up instead and waited until he got off the phone so we could talk. After the phone conversation was over, he grabbed his leather briefcase and walked over to where I was washing dishes.

"Ryan, I can't wait for this weekend, baby," I said happily.

"You deserve it and more. I'm going to treat you like the queen that you are," he whispered in my ear before giving me a goodbye kiss and walking out the door.

Since Ryan had been working day and night, we hardly had any time to spend together, so he and I had finally decided to do something special this weekend and head to Miami. I was super excited about that because the last time I had gone to Miami was about five years ago. I was ready for the sun to hit my skin and have sex on the beach.

I had just finished cleaning up the kitchen when my phone began to ring. When I looked down and noticed that it was my brother, I started not to answer it because he only called when he wanted something. I knew either he wanted to beg me or he wanted me to do him a favor, but I decided to answer just to make sure he was okay.

"Sup, Dre."

"Shed, what you got going on?" he asked.

"Boy, what do you want?" I muttered into the phone as I turned on the TV in the living room.

"Damn, what's wrong with you? You acting like you ain't glad to hear from me."

I rolled my eyes because this nigga just didn't know.

"I need to hold your car."

I became silent.

"Sis, you there?"

I knew I should haven't picked up the damn phone. I took a deep breath and counted to ten.

"Nigga, when you need to hold it?"

"Two days from now. My big homie gets out the pin this week. He going to need someone to pick him up."

"I guess … but you better put some damn gas back in."

"Thanks, sis, you the best."

"You're welcome. Can you do me a favor?"

"Yeah, what you need, sis?"

"Can you come stay with Ashanti and Malcolm while Ryan and I go out of town?"

"Yeah, you know I got you. I will watch them."

When the call was disconnected, I smiled to myself as I thought about my little brother Andre. He could be so annoying at times and knew exactly how to work my nerves, but I'd go to the end of the world for him. After our parents got a divorce, my dad left us for his new family. My mom had to fend for me and my brother the best way she knew how. Things were great at first, but when she lost her job, we had to eventually move to the worst part of Albany. She was never home because she was always out scheming and hustling to take care of us. I was only thirteen and took it upon myself to look after Andre when she was nowhere to be found.

Tears began to fall from my eyes as I thought back to the day when I received a knock on my front door.

Andre and I had just gotten home from school when the police came to my house and told me that my mother had been murdered. I lost sense of reality when I heard that because I was only a child myself. I didn't know where my life was headed, and every little ounce of security was taken away from me. The fact that my mother wasn't close to any of her relatives left Andre and me to be put in the system. I didn't want to go to foster care, but we had no other choice. I wasn't of legal age to take care of my brother and myself with no help. The state tried to separate us, but my life changed when my Uncle Leo decided to step in.

At first, I thought my uncle was sent from heaven and was rescuing us from the hell that we were probably going to endure in foster care, but it wasn't long before I realized that the state had made a horrible mistake. The state had really fucked up when they released me and my little brother to my uncle, who was an undercover pervert. As soon as Andre and I had gotten settled into his house, he started to creep inside my room every other night and touch me in places his nasty hands had no business touching. He used to whisper in my ear dirty things that still brought chills to my body when I thought back to my past.

He always promised that he was going to make me a woman before I turned eighteen, and I swear that was the sickest shit that I had ever heard of. I was his dead sister's first-born daughter, and it disgusted me that he was actually trying to put his nasty dick inside me.

After I had enough of trying to fight Leon off of me, I packed me and Andre's shit and ran away from his ass. We had only been staying with him for two years but there was no way I was going to be able to make it until I turned legal age. I had no clue where Andre and I were going to end up, and I didn't care as long as we were away from that house.

I had saved up a little money while I was living with Uncle Leo. I constantly did my chores without him asking and for that he would give me pocket money the entire time I was living with him. I never spent a dime of that money because I knew one day hard times was going to come and I was going to need it. I was somewhat prepared to run away but the money only lasted so long before I was broke, yet again.

One night, Andre and I were at the Waffle House trying to figure out how to get up some money to eat, when I ran into this nigga named Mecca. He took me and my brother in and freed us from our problems.

Mecca was a straight up a hood ghetto pimp. He was a skinny dude with curly hair, chocolate in complexion, with freckles all over his face. Yeah, this nigga was a real pretty boy, but he would still would whoop a hoe's ass. Andre and Mecca got along very well. He used to take him out and show Andre how to survive in the streets if he ever had to. All I wanted to do was be able to finish high school so I could graduate, get a job, and be able to provide for me and Andre. By me only being fifteen, Mecca supported my decision and always kept me motivated to be the best that I could be.

After I finished high school, Andre had gotten so far in the streets, running with gangs, and involving himself with petty crimes. There was nothing that I could really do, and after a while of trying to talk with him, I eventually gave up and decided it was best to let him find his own way. We always stayed in touch with each other, even though I didn't agree with his lifestyle. When I turned eighteen, Mecca ended up getting locked up. I was faced with figuring out how I was going to survive yet again, which sent me into a deeper depression, but I wasn't depressed for very long before one of Mecca's girls got me on as a bartender at a club called Big Daddy. Mecca's girl really looked out for me and sat me up with a nigga who made me a fake ID because I had to be twenty-one to serve drinks.

I didn't complain about the pay because some money was better than no money at all. I was only working a part-time job, mixing drinks, three days out the week. At first, I came to work on time, mixed the best drinks in the town, and got paid. On the days that I was off, I would get wasted and sleep the day away. Eventually, all the alcohol began to affect my work ethic, and I began to start coming to work late due to me suffering from hangovers. Finally, I was fired. Three days after I was fired, I swear my life kept throwing stones at my ass because I started to have bad luck.

I remember stepping off the bus and walking towards my apartment complex when I noticed my complex was on fire. Smoke engulfed the streets, and the sound of the fire truck was growing louder as they got closer to my street. I stood across the street as tears began to run down my face. I wiped the tears from my eyes as I watched the firefighters put the fire out. I was grateful to learn that no one was hurt, but once I heard the whispers about my top neighbor's bad ass kids who always liked to play with matches, had started the fire, I was beyond pissed off. I was planning on coming home from job hunting to hop in the tub so I could relax, but none of that shit happened. I was with no job and no place to sleep, which led me to walk the streets until my legs grew tired. When I woke up the next morning, I was in a motel room half naked and didn't remember how in the hell I had gotten there. I hopped out the bed and immediately tried to find my clothes, but my head was hurting so damn bad that I could barely concentrate.

The door swung open and this black man who looked like a gorilla stepped in with a devilish smirk on this face. He told me his name was Geno. He was dressed like a cheap ass pimp with two dusty white women on his arms. I was lost and was still trying to figure out how in the hell I had ended up in this motel room. He quickly filled me in on just how I had gotten there, and I was beyond disgusted. He claimed I owed him my life for saving me and taking me off the streets. I felt sick to my stomach, and when I looked around the motel and noticed a bunch of drugs lying around, I wanted to leave, but how Geno was looking, I knew deep down he was never going to let me go. For two years, I worked the streets and did drugs heavily before I finally got the opportunity to leave.

The only reason I had a chance to get away from his ass was because one of the hoes he was pimping out had killed his ass. When I learned that Geno was dead, that was the best day of my life. I was finally free, but I was a dope fiend, always looking for my next hit. Six months later after Geno's death, I checked myself into rehab and got myself clean.

The type of lifestyle that I lived before Ryan entered my life was never spoken of. Ryan knew nothing about my past, and I was planning on keeping it that way.

The ringing of my cell brought me back to the present, and I quickly picked up the phone when I saw Ryan's name.

"Hey, baby," I said happily into the phone.

"Baby, I'm sorry, but we ain't going to be able to go on our little getaway. I have to fly to Boston this weekend; it's a work emergency. I promise I will make it up to you."

My whole heart felt as if it had been pulled out my chest and crushed with a hammer. I was truly looking forward to going on this trip. I ended the call as hot tears began to form in my eyes. I was pissed off because every time Ryan and I made plans to do something together, shit always seemed to come up at the last minute. I couldn't do nothing but wipe the tears from my eyes, as I stared at the four walls like a dumb ass.

CHAMP

"Room 244 top; it's time to roll it up!" the officer yelled as he unlocked my cell door. I had been dreaming about this day for about nine years.

"Alright!" I yelled, grabbing my manila envelope that had contained a few of my personal pictures. All the other shit didn't matter to me.

When I stepped out my cell, my heart was finally relieved. I had been gone from my family and the streets for a very long time. As soon as I came down the stairs, I was greeted by a dude that meant a lot to me.

"The day has finally come for you, young brother," Monster said, giving me a brotherly hug.

Monster was my big homie. He taught me how to survive in prison. Monster, whose real name was Victor Peen, was currently serving a life sentence. He explained to me the way he got his nickname when we first met, and I was speechless as he told me the story. He was only thirty-five, but he had been locked up since he was sixteen. Georgia didn't play with you on giving you your time. All bullshit to the side, he was a good-hearted dude if he rocked with you. Now if you crossed him, you would really see that crazy side. On the real though, if it wasn't for Monster, I probably would have been serving a life sentence, so I have much respect for the nigga for stepping in on the day I was close to murdering a few niggas for coming at me like I was some type of punk.

It was one of them days that a nigga just didn't feel like being bothered. My girl had just written me telling me she loved me, but she wasn't in love with me anymore. I was in my fucking feelings after I read that shit. I mean, reading that really had my mind fucked up because I wasn't even expecting to hear that shit. The fact that I had risked my freedom to make sure she was on top and had everything her heart desired was what hurt me the most. I felt betrayed, and I was furious. I didn't want to speak to nobody; I just wanted to be left alone. One thing I hated was when people didn't keep their word or lied to me, because nobody deserved that shit. After I finished reading her letter, I quickly balled it up and went ham in my cell. I grabbed all her letters that she had ever written me, and tore each of them into tiny pieces. If I could have, I would have lit them bitches on fire. She was dead to me, and I didn't want to have shit to do with her. I grabbed my music player and began to try to calm my nerves as I listened to me a little music, but that still didn't help me, so I decided to work out. I worked out for over an hour straight, but the pain was still there.

The more I tried forgetting her, the more her image appeared in my head. When I was on my first set of pull-ups, these two lame ass dudes stepped in my way, and I politely asked them to move. I guess these two pussy niggas were in there feelings also because they started to pop off at the mouth. I wasn't the type to fuck around with these fake ass niggas around here, so I headed back to my cell, lifted up my mattress, and got my Shelia. Shelia was my problem-solving weapon. She was this long metal iron that was sharpened on the tip. She had been in my possession for almost two years and never had I ever had a chance to use her. I was just about to head back to find the two niggas who tried me, but that was when Monster appeared and talked some sense into me. If it wasn't for him, I wouldn't be getting out today.

An hour later, I was officially free and the prison gates had closed behind me. It felt so good to be free, and I was glad to finally be out of prison. Finally, my dream had come true. The air smelled so fresh as it ran through my nostrils. Hearing the different styles of how people was talking filled my ear as I rode the bus to my destination. I stared out the bus window and couldn't help but notice the multimillion dollar buildings flashing before my eyes. For the last nine years, I had seen nothing but the same old blue brick building and prison gates every single day. That was a very depressing sight to see for nine years, but some type of way, with the grace of God, I got through it. There was no word that could describe the feeling that I was feeling at this very moment. I had to catch the bus because my partner said he wasn't about to come across them prison lines. I respected that because I promised myself I would never bring my ass near a prison ever again. The ride on the bus wasn't bad, and it wasn't long before I had finally arrived at the bus station. I stepped off the bus and saw my pea head homie, Dre.

"Damn! Nigga, you done got huge!" Dre laughed as he gave me some dap.

When I came to prison, I was only about 150 pounds. Now I was 210 with the mind frame of doing what was right. Most people probably remembered me as a young wild ass dude with dreads hanging down past my shoulders. Now I was rocking the low fade with mad waves. Before I came to prison, I didn't care about nothing, but I was a changed man and I wanted something out of life. I had a daughter to think about.

"Yeah, I ain't have shit to do but workout and read a shit load of books," I joked as I opened the passenger door and hopped inside Dre's candy apple red Lexus.

"This you, bruh?"

I couldn't help but admire his new whip.

"Hell naw, I wish, but this my big head ass sister's whip." He chuckled as he started up the engine.

"Shed, your sis riding good," I said as I checked out the white leather interior as Dre pulled out of the bus station and headed to Albany.

Even though Dre and I had been homies before I got locked up, never had I ever met his damn sister. Every time I would come over to see him, she was never there. He always would tell me she was at school or out with friends. Dre was a real street nigga but he always kept his street life away from his sister, and I respected that shit, because I was sure I would have been the same if I had a sister too.

"So, what's the move around town? I want to know has Albany changed since the last time I was there."

"Same old shit; niggas still getting popped and these ratchets hoes are more ratchet," he revealed as he turned right on Radford Boulevard, then made a quick left on Dawson Road.

"That's why I'm leaving the streets where they at," I assured him with strong emphasis.

"So, are you talking about you going to get a nine to five?" he asked sarcastically.

"If I have to. Shed, I have a daughter that needs taken care of."

Dre didn't say nothing, just nodded his head in agreement. I could tell my response made him feel some type of way. Andre and I had mad history together. Before I got locked up, we had started a small clique called EME. We did everything from rob the pizza man, shoot at anybody that wasn't part of the team, shoplift, fuck different hoes together, and anything that would put money in our pockets. I was only eighteen then with no sense of what my future held for me. Now Andre and I were thirty and it was time to put all that childish shit behind us. No longer was I going to be doing the same shit that I was doing in my teens. If Andre felt what I felt, he would understand when I told him I was done with the streets.

"I know you might have had other plans, but I'm going to do everything to stay out and keep my nose clean," I uttered as I stared at my daughter, Faith's, picture.

"Yeah, I understand, bruh. I did picture us taking over Albany again, that's all," Dre murmured.

To be honest, I didn't really care if Andre was mad or not. There was no way I was about to go back to the pin for anyone. None of the crew that Andre and I were running with put money on my books. I learned the hard way that there were no such things as loyalty in these streets.

"So, what are your plans?" Dre asked curiously.

"To be honest, I'm definitely not about to work at no fast food joint, and I know I can't get no corporate job because of this damn record I got. But I don't want that shit anyway because I ain't the type of nigga who wants to dress up in a suit and tie every damn day. What I do love is working out every day, so I'm thinking about becoming a personal trainer or some shit like that."

Dre had a perplexed look on his face.

"Personal trainer," he said with sarcasm.

He looked at me then back out the window.

Damn, he acts like I said some impossible shit, I thought to myself. I didn't even bother by Dre and his feelings; instead, I kept rubbing my daughter's face as I stared down at her most recent picture.

I knew deep down in my heart that Dre wasn't feeling the decisions that I was planning on making to improve my life. At this point in time in my life, I didn't care what people thought of me. At the end of the day, the only person opinion who I truly cared about was my daughter. Right before I got locked up, Trina had just told me that she was pregnant with my child. I dreamed every night of the day that I was actually going to be able to hold my baby in my arms. If Trina didn't do nothing else while I was locked up, she sent pictures of my daughter at least twice a month. The only thing that she didn't allow Faith to do was come visit me, and I respected her decision.

I was nervous as hell when Dre pulled up at Trina's apartment complex.

"Nigga, you sure you going to be good here?" Dre asked.

"Yeah, thanks for the lift."

"You know I got your back, homie. Well, let me get this car back to my sis and I will hit you up later."

I nodded my head as he reached over and dapped me up.

Trina stayed on the Northside of Albany in a complex called West wind. It was mostly young parents and single mothers trying to raise their kids who lived in these apartments. Trina had told me in her last letter that I could crash at her place until I got back on my feet. I wasn't planning on being there long, but I was grateful that she took a nigga in when he had no other place to go.

I took a deep breath and exhaled. I stepped to apartment F2 and knocked on the door. My heart began to beat erratically in my chest. I could feel the sweat dripping off my nose as I waited for someone to open the door. I could hear footsteps coming to the door and when the door opened a few seconds later, Trina's raspberry perfume invaded my nostril. Trina stood there looking real gorgeous, I couldn't lie about that. I know my heart paused for a brief second, and I was stuck with nothing to say. Trina was wearing a cut off top with tight gray shorts and some white socks.

Damn, I thought to myself as I took her all in.

Trina was five feet, very dark chocolate complexion, 145 pounds, with long, jet-black hair that stopped midway down her back. She had a pretty oval face with very deep dimples, brown round bug eyes that were sexy as hell, bright white teeth, and a glow about her that could light up the room when was stepped in. I could tell she must have been working out because her body looked toned. As I looked at her, I noticed she had a flat stomach and appeared to have a couple of abs as well. She still had a great massive ass that I bet had niggas going crazy over her.

"Heyyy, Champ!" she greeted, opening the door for me to step inside.

"Hey, Trina," I replied, walking in and giving her a firm hug. Damn, she was smelling good as hell and her body felt super soft. I looked down into her eyes and was hooked. My mind was telling me to let her go, but my body was saying something totally different. Trina closed the door with her foot before she did something that I wasn't expecting. When her lips touched my lips, I was in shock, but I wasn't going to be the type of nigga who was going to pull away. Her lips were still as smooth and soft as I had remembered. I dropped everything that I was holding in my hands and it fell to the floor. My hands weren't shy because they were under her shirt with a quickness. I touched and played with her nipples as I placed soft kisses on her neck. She pushed me down on the couch, unfastened my pants, and grabbed a fistful of my dick. I mean a nigga was already on hard and ready to fuck some, if she was down to give me some ass. She brushed her hair to the side as she began to stroke her hand up and down in a steady motion.

"You know I missed this dick," she admitted as she kissed all over my ten-inch gorilla dick. I just closed my eyes and bit down on my bottom lip as her mouth covered my dick.

"Mmmmmm, shit!" I moaned as I stared into her brown eyes.

She smiled as she continued to work her magic on me. When her mouth wrapped around my dick, I almost lost all sense of myself. This was the best head ever, and I was enjoying the shit. I eased my hand across her head as I pushed her head farther down on my dick. Trina stared right into my soul as she continued to suck me off. She came up for air, stood up, and took off her shorts. I bent her ass over the couch as I spread open her ass cheeks and displayed her pretty shaved pussy. One thing about Trina, she was naturally wet all the damn time; never was she the type of female that had a nigga waiting for some pussy. As I slid my tongue inside her warm wetness, I took my right hand and spread open her ass cheeks so I could get deeper inside her. She tasted sweeter than honey. My tongue went in and out making sure to make love to her insides.

"Mmmm ... Shhhhh ... Shhhh!" she moaned out as my tongue flicked across her clit. I shoved my whole face between her cheeks while she screamed out my name.

"Damn, Champ, shit!" Trina screamed out.

Just when I thought I was about to get me some pussy, she turned around with an expression that threw me off. She pulled away from me which left a nigga confused.

"We can't do this."

I watched as she began to put her clothes back on. The fact she was moaning my name just a second ago and now she was acting cold and distant didn't sit well with me.

I grabbed her arm because I wanted to know what was up with her. My dick was rock hard and I was sexually frustrated.

"What wrong with you?" I asked Trina.

"Champ, this not right."

I was trying to approach her, but she put her hand up and shook her head.

"Much as I want to take it there with you, I can't," she said before she stormed into her bedroom.

I was left there with a fucking hard-on and was too angry to even do anything about it.

Instead of begging for some pussy, I fixed my clothes and flopped down on the couch. I could still taste her on my damn tongue. "Damn," I said to myself.

I looked around and noticed just how nice and neat Trina's apartment looked. She had a leather black living room set, 50-inch flat screen TV, wooden bookshelves, crystal nightstand with pictures of her and Faith, and a white tiger print rug hanging on the wall. I wasn't even going to lie; over the years, Trina had stepped her game up and was doing good for herself. I still remembered the day I met her.

I was coming out of Bill Miller's gym, and the sun was beaming down on my face. It was hot as hell as I walked behind the gym to grab my bike. When I noticed it was gone, I began to get irritated because I thought it was one of my partners who didn't have shit else to do but fuck with me. It was way too hot that day to be on some fuck shit. I decided to head back in the gym to see if I spotted one of my partners, but none of them were anywhere to be found. I was pissed the hell off and was just about to head back outside when I saw her.

"Does this bike belong to you?" a girl asked as she placed one hand on her hip.

"Yes, that's mine," I choked out.

I almost forgot all about that damn bike as I stared back at the beautiful girl standing before me.

She handed me over my gray and white mountain bike and was just about to walk away when I called out to her.

"What's your name?" I asked.

"Trina," she gently said as she showed off her pretty white teeth.

"Can I walk you home?"

"I don't mine," Trina replied gently.

We walked around the whole neighborhood until the sun began to go down. As we walked, we talked about her life story and she didn't hold anything back about herself. I learned she was the second oldest out of her siblings, she had two brothers and one sister, her parents were still together, and they had been married since she was born. She also told me that when she got older that she wanted to become a judge because she wanted to make a difference in people's lives. I looked at Trina as a girl that was different than all the rest I had come in contact with. She was special, and we had an instant connection that I knew was different. That night, I made Trina my girlfriend, and I felt it was the best decision that I had ever made. I was young, but I was deeply in love with her.

Knock, Knock.

I was pulled from my thoughts of Trina and I, as the knocking on Trina's front door became louder. I groaned as I slid off the couch and headed towards the front door. When I opened the door, my heart sunk to the bottom of my chest as my stomach did a major flip. I couldn't believe what I actually saw standing before my eyes.

SASHA

RYAN'S BIG TRIP

As I walked Ryan to his white BMW, my heart was still crushed. I had planned the whole weekend in Miami, and now I had to go and unpack all my clothes because, apparently, I wasn't going anywhere. I was disappointed, but I knew it wasn't anything that I could really do about it. I looked up at Ryan and gave him a half a smile as he loaded his luggage inside the trunk. He turned in my direction and pulled me towards him.

"Baby, I'm sorry I had to cancel at the last minute. I promise I will make it up to you," he whispered as he placed a kiss on my forehead.

"It's okay," I lied.

Deep down inside, it wasn't okay. I wanted to slap the shit out of him because I had been planning for weeks for this trip. Over the years I had been with Ryan, he had cancelled a lot of our trips because of his work.

As I followed him to the driver's side of his car, he gave me the number to his hotel if I couldn't reach him on his cell. He kept apologizing for the weekend, but I didn't even respond to any of it. I just nodded my head, even though my heart felt as if it had been ripped out my chest. I kissed him gently on his lips and told him to drive safely. He promised to contact me when his flight landed. I knew how to play my role, so I tried my best not to let him see that I was hurting inside. I was a fraud and smiled in his face as I closed his car door. I stood in the middle of the road and watched as his car disappeared down the busy street.

My life felt as if it was missing something. I always felt alone, even though I was married with two kids. I had the perfect life, the perfect husband and kids, but I still felt as if I needed more to fill this void that I felt inside. I closed my eyes as I said a silent prayer to the Lord and asked him why I still wasn't happy with the life that I was living.

"Ma," Ashanti called out to me.

I opened my eyes and noticed my daughter standing at the front door waiting for me to come back inside the house. Ashanti and I were the only two at home. Malcolm was hanging at his friend's house and was going to come home later that night.

"Yes, baby, what you want?" I asked Ashanti as I walked over to where she was standing with my front door wide open. She had my cell phone in her hand and handed it to me.

"Ms. Sweet Pea on the phone; she wants to talk to you."

I grabbed the phone from my daughter and kissed her on her cheek.

"Thanks, baby."

"Wassup, girl," I spoke into the phone as I walked into the house and locked the door behind me.

"What you up to, girl?"

"Nun."

"I thought you was supposed to be sipping drinks and having sex on the beach in Miami," Sweet Pea joked.

"Chile, you know Mr. Ryan had some other shit going on so we couldn't go. It was work related, so he had to fly out of town to Boston."

"Well, you know how that is. Do you have any other plans since that didn't go through?"

"Nall, I'm sitting home with Ashanti, looking crazy."

"Let's go catch a movie together tonight at eight."

I agreed to head out with her, but told her to give me an hour for Ashanti to get dressed. When I told Ashanti that we were going to have a girl's night out and we were going to the movies, Ashanti was excited and quickly ran in her room to get dressed. I made sure to send Tamara a text message letting her know I was leaving the house to head to the movies, and I was going to pick up Malcolm when I returned.

I jumped in the shower to freshen myself up, and once I stepped out, I grabbed something comfortable to wear. I decided to rock a gray Nike Shirt, black tights, and my all white Air Max. I had my hair slicked down and pulled back from my face. When I had made it downstairs, Ashanti was waiting on me. She looked so adorable with her hair braided in a Mohawk with her black Polo shirt, a pair of khaki Polo shorts, and a pair of black flats.

"Are you ready to ride out?"

"Yes, Mom, I'm ready."

I smiled as I grabbed my keys and purse and headed towards the car.

Within minutes, we were arriving at Sweet Pea's house. Sweet Pea stayed in the most drug infested area in Albany. I hated coming over to her place at night because shit was always going down after the street light came on. The fact that Sweet Pea had a pretty decent job working at Bell South, the phone company, I always pressured her about moving, but Sweet Pea was stubborn as hell and always made an excuse why she couldn't move. Sweet Pea was living in a three-bedroom home with a fence going around her house. But we all knew these street niggas could easily hop over the fence and rob her ass if they wanted to. However, Sweet Pea never had any problems with anyone robbing or trying to harm her so that was one of the reasons why she didn't think she should move. Her ass drove around town with a brand-new black Toyota and she had just gotten some rims on it. I blew my horn to let her know I was outside and I was ready to go. I noticed a few niggas posted up by her fence, smoking them a fat ass blunt. The weed was strong as hell and had me about to damn choke. I quickly rolled up my window when Ashanti asked me what that stinky smell was.

When Sweet Pea stepped out the house, I could see the smirk on her face. She threw up her hand to the niggas who was smoking by her fence before she hopped into my car. Sweet Pea was a plus-sized chick with a very cute face, but I swear this bitch didn't know how to dress. She was rocking a black dress that stopped at her knee, a blue jean jacket, and high-rise boots. She had her hair blown out and wrapped in a shoe string. I just shook my head and mouthed to Ashanti to "be nice."

"Hey, y'all," Sweet Pea blurted out as she flopped down in her the seat.

Ashanti waved and went back to looking at her tablet.

"Wassup, girl," I said as I backed out her driveway. Right before I could put the gear in drive, her so-called baby daddy, Rodney, came to the door with his shirt off. I guess he was trying to see who she was leaving with.

Sweet Pea and Rodney had been talking for about five years off and on. When I first met Rodney's dusty ass, I told her from the jump that he was going to be an issue, but Sweet Pea wouldn't listen to anything I said. Rodney had dragged her ass through the mud, but Sweet Pea was still holding onto the nigga, even when he was dragging her down. He didn't work because he was on disability because he had fallen off a forklift at work. I had no issue with Rodney not being able to work, but the issue came in when he started receiving his disability check. He gets his check on the first, but Sweet Pea wouldn't see his ass until he was about broke. Rodney was nothing but a straight up crackhead. I had heard so many rumors around town about what he does to get high. Onc time I got up the nerve to ask Sweet Pea why she stayed with Rodney knowing that all he did was get high when he got his check and didn't help her with any bills. She only told me that she stayed because of the kids they had together.

They had some beautiful twin girls, and I used to tease her all the time. I used to tell her that the hospital had given her the wrong babies because them twins were way too gorgeous to come from Rodney's black ass.

"Girl, I have something to tell you," Sweet Pea gushed.

Her face lit up like a Christmas tree, so I knew whatever she had to tell me was good news.

"I met this dude and we been kicking it hard as fuck."

"What about Rodney?" I asked like his ass was really a threat or something.

"Fuck him. I'm so tired of him that it doesn't make any sense."

"I been told you to not fuck with him. So what you going to do about the other dude?" I asked her curiously.

When she told me that the nigga she was talking to was married, I didn't say nothing at first because Sweet Pea knew how I felt about that type of shit. She told me that they hadn't had sex, but they had been texting a lot lately. As she went on and on talking about this married man, I zoned her out as I began to think about Ryan. I began to wonder if he could be messing around on me. All types of scenarios about Ryan began to play out in my mind. But what really threw me over the edge was when Sweet Pea told me that her and the married man was supposed to be making plans to go out of town. My mind went on overdrive as I began to really stress the issue of Ryan going all the way to Boston on such short notice. I began to wonder if he had flown all the way to Boston on business like he led me to believe, or was it something more that I had missed. I was in my feelings, but I made sure that Sweet Pea didn't notice.

When we arrived at the movie theater, the parking lot was packed as hell, and it took me forever it seemed to find a parking spot. We stood in line close to ten minutes before we got the tickets and headed inside towards the concession stand. Sweet Pea ordered her a big bucket of popcorn with extra butter, a large strawberry drink, and some baked bean candies. Ashanti wasn't a big eater, but when it came to junk food, I had to keep my eye on her because she could eat you out a house and a home. I ordered her a small popcorn and a small Hi-C. I only ordered me a bottle water and a pack of Lemon Heads. I wasn't about to eat all that greasy shit because I was trying to watch my figure, plus, I loved me some damn Lemon Heads; them bitches be good as hell. When I turned around from the concession stand, my heart nearly stopped.

"Well ... Well ... Who do we have here?" Geno asked with a devilish smirk on his face.

I thought I was seeing a ghost because I should have sworn this nigga was killed by one of his hoes years ago, but here he stood, and he was very much alive.

"I thought you was dead," I uttered as I took a step back.

He chuckled evilly, as he took a step towards me.

"Sasha! Who is this?" Sweet Pea asked with a perplexed look on her face.

At that moment, I had totally forgot that Sweet Pea and Ashanti were even near me.

"He's an old friend," I tried to convince myself as well as them.

I took Ashanti by her arm as I tried to walk off, but Geno grabbed me with a tight firm grip by my arm.

"Let go of my mama!" Ashanti yelled out.

"Geno, let me go!" I demanded angrily.

"Bitch, you owe me some money!"

His grip felt as if it was stopping my blood flow. By this time, a crowd began to form around us. I was so embarrassed that this was actually happening to me. I tried to snatch away from him, but this time he pulled me towards him. His breath smelled like a bag of onion which made me want to vomit over his alligator shoes.

"The lady said let her go," the deep voice said.

Geno stared down at me and turned to whoever had just stepped in to intervene. I caressed the bruise that was left on my arm from where he gripped me way too tightly.

"Look, bruh, I don't want to have to hurt you," the dude replied.

"You a bold ass nigga to step in Geno's business," Geno raved as he stepped in the man's face.

"The best thing you can do is get out my damn face," the man warned Geno.

Geno just had that evil smirk on this face like he wasn't scared of shit. Geno glanced around him like he was about to walk off before he took a swing at the man, but the man must have known what Geno was up to because the man side stepped and threw a quick jab, hitting Geno on the side of his face, which made Geno stumble and lose his balance.

When Geno charged the man, the man blocked every single punch that Geno sent his way. By this time, the crowd was cheering the two men on and some were even recording it on Facebook live. The man quickly gave Geno two right licks to the face and one to the stomach before Geno was laid out on the floor. I closed Ashanti's eyes because I didn't want her to see any of this, but at the same time, I was happy as hell that Geno was getting his ass kicked. He was getting everything he deserved. The man was just about to stomp his ass when the police busted through the door.

"Freeze!" the white, fat police officer screamed waving his gun in the air.

The man raised his hand in the air and dropped to the ground. Geno was out laid out, holding on to his stomach in pain. Just when they walked over to arrest the man who had stepped in and saved me, I knew it was time I spoke up.

"Officer!" I yelled, as I walked towards him.

"Ma'am, please take a step back," the police instructed.

"The man you are trying to arrest was only protecting himself," I slowly said, looking in the officer's eyes.

The crowd joined in and said the same thing. The officer looked back at me then looked back at the crowd.

"Well, son, this is your lucky day," he told the man before he decided to let the man go.

"But you, my friend, is about to take a ride downtown," the officer assured Geno.

The officer wrote down the man's information, and I gave the officer mine as a witness. The crowd began clapping as the police officer took Geno away.

"Daddy!" A sweet voice caught my attention.

The man and his daughter embraced each other in a tight hug as the crowd cheered in the distance. As they were walking away, I looked over at Sweet Pea as she nodded her head at me.

I ran to catch up to the stranger who had come to my defense.

He was tall, muscular, dark chocolate in complexion, and was rocking a low fade with waves.

"Excuse me!" I yelled towards the man.

He turned around and looked at me. His daughter held onto his hand as she stared back at me with her pretty brown eyes.

"I just want to tell you thank you for what you did back there."

"No problem," he assured me.

"My name is Sasha, and what's yours?

"My name is Champ," he mumbled before he vanished into the crowd.

CHAMP

A MONTH LATER

Shit was going good for me, and I was enjoying my new job working at Tony's Gym. Even though I didn't have a client booked yet, I still felt like something was going to change. I had ads posted everywhere on Facebook, IG, and other sites. I wasn't going to give up. I was going to continue grinding and saving my checks so I could get my own place. Trina and Jerome weren't tripping, but a man like myself needed my own spot. Most nights, I stayed over my brother Jerome's crib with him and his family. Jerome was my older brother that was strictly about his business. He worked for this company called Coat and Clark. He had been out there for forever. Jerome and I were the complete opposite. Growing up, I was mostly in the streets while he was stuck with his nose in a book. He was the type of dude that did no wrong and never went out to the club, smoked week, or even let a drop of alcohol touch his lips. He lived his life very simple. He went to work five days a week, came home to take care of his wife, and attended churched every time the church door opened on Sunday mornings.

After serving all that time in prison, now I understood where he was coming from. I wished I would have been more like him growing up. Jerome was married to this woman named Karen. She was down to earth and worked at an insurance company called Nationwide. They had two pretty little girls named Jada and Tiffany. They were so adorable and kept me laughing all day long. They always ran up to me every time they saw me to ask me how did I like prison. I always made sure to sit them down and explain to each of them that they would never want to go there.

"Daddy!" Faith shouted my name as she walked into the living room.

On the nights that I wasn't staying with Jerome, I was over at Trina's place with my daughter, Faith. I hadn't really been around Trina since the first day I came back home and she decided that us fucking would only complicate shit. Turns out she was dating some nigga, so on the days that I stayed over her house, she would always pack her shit and go stay with her man. I didn't sweat it; as long as long as I could chill with Faith, I was good. Faith and I had gotten so close it was unbelievable. She took my attitude from me, but when she wanted to figure something out, she would sit back and observe everything in the room. She got that trait from Trina because Trina always did that shit. I swear I could never get nothing past Trina when she and I were together.

"Yes, Faith!" I yelled out.

I always made sure to respect Trina's place. I never went roaming in her bedrooms or tried snooping around. I wasn't that type of nigga to be asking her all these crazy ass questions about her personal business either.

I gestured for Faith to come sit beside me on the couch.

"Tell me what's wrong, Faith."

"When you and mommy get married, can I be the flower girl?" Faith asked gently.

"Huh?" I wasn't expecting to hear no shit like that.

"Lily was a flower girl at her parents' wedding. So, Daddy, can I be a flower girl?" she asked as she stared in directly in my eyes.

"Well..."

"Pleasssseeee..." she begged.

My heart wasn't built to destroy her dream.

"One day, baby, you can be that flower girl."

I couldn't break her heart and tell her that there was no way in hell that Trina and I were ever getting back together. Trina and I had a good mutual relationship; we both knew where each other stood in each other life. When we were together, it was a fun time. She wanted more than I was willing to give at that time. I just was craving the street life at the time, and Trina wanted me to put a ring on her finger. I wasn't ready for all that.

I started cleaning Trina's apartment because I didn't want her to come home and get all in her feelings about her apartment being messy. So to keep down confusion, I made sure to fix the place up like she liked it.

THE NEXT MORNING

Faith was coming from the back room wearing her school uniform. I made sure to hand her a few dollars so she could pay for her lunch. I wiped down the kitchen table, TV, picture frames, and other things that needed to be wiped down. I headed towards the kitchen and began washing the dishes that Faith had messed up the night before. I had cooked Faith some baked chicken, green beans, rice, and homemade biscuits the night before. One thing I knew was how to cook a decent meal. As I stared at the fridge, I saw a picture of Trina and Faith. Just seeing that picture brought great joy to my heart. All the wrong I had done over the years when I was out in the streets, I still couldn't believe that God had blessed me with Faith.

My cell began to vibrate in my pocket, and I quickly dug it out to answer it.

"Hello."

"You need to stop all that," Trina joked.

"What I do?" I asked.

"You up here trying to sound all sexy."

I chuckled.

"So, you think my voice sounds sexy?" I asked her curiously.

"Uh, no." She shot me down hard. "Boy, are you up, and is Faith ready to go to school?"

"Yeah, she up and ready."

"Okay, give me five minutes and I will be over there to pick her up."

She didn't even give me time to respond before she ended the call.

Once the house was spotless and the kitchen was clean, I quickly hopped in the shower so I could start getting ready for the day. I had a lot of shit to do today, such as going to Dre's sister crib with him, go pick up my check and cash it, and go search for me an apartment. When I finally emerged from the bathroom, Trina was coming through the front door. I only had a towel wrapped around my waist as water dripped down my chest. Our eyes locked on one another for a brief second. I could tell she was admiring a nigga because it took her a minute to look away.

"Yeah, I been working out. I got to keep these abs tight," I teased her.

Trina was looking sexy as usual. I couldn't deny that shit. She was sporting a navy blue Louis Vuitton jumper. She was still going to school during the weekend and worked part time with a lawyer.

She gestured for Faith to hurry up so she wouldn't be late for school. Faith ran up to me and gave me a hug before following Trina out the front door. When they left, I grabbed my phone so I could call Dre.

"Yo," Dre answered with his loud music playing in the background.

"What's good, bruh? What time you coming through?"

"Shed! Give me about five or ten minutes. I got to stop by Walgreens on the corner of Dawson Road to grab my cousin a Green Dot Money Pak card so he can enjoy his birthday."

"I understand, nigga, because when you locked down, that card comes in handy, especially if it's a long weekend. The two meals they feed you on the weekend don't be hitting on shit," I said into the phone.

"Bet."

I hung up and started to put on some clothes. I was rocking a black and red t-shirt with the word Faith going across it, denim jeans, black Air Force, and a Raider's fitted cap. I did a double take, making sure I had everything I needed because I didn't have time to be coming back because I had forgot some shit. I locked up the apartment and was headed down the stairs and was almost at the bottom when I began to smell a strong scent of burning rubber. I could recognize the smell of crack a mile away. It was quiet as hell outside, and all them bad ass kids must had went to school today because when they were home, they'd be deep outside and be about to knock your ass down with their rough playing. I had just made it to the middle of the courtyard when I heard someone call out my name.

"Champ!" a sexy voice yelled out to me.

I turned around and there stood Roshika.

Roshika was a chick who stayed in front of Trina's apartment. She and I had been messing around from time to time, since I had gotten back home. I knew I was playing a crazy ass game, but Trina wouldn't fuck a nigga, so I had to get it from somewhere. The fact that Trina had her life and I had mine, I felt like she wouldn't care what I did. The only thing Trina and I had in common was Faith. We never got on anything personal, and we always kept our conversations short and simple.

"Wassup, shawty," I said, walking on her porch.

She smiled seductively as she licked on the cherry Blow Pop in her mouth. She was a natural born freak, and she was always down to ride and suck a dick. She stood at five feet six inches tall, with dark skin and an oval face with silver piercings in both dimples. She rocked long dreads, and she had a body that made a blind man crave his vision back. She was the type of chick that actually had an hourglass body and knew what to do to pull niggas.

"When you going to lay some of that dick on a bitch again?"

"Well ... a nigga been tied up."

"Look, my birthday this weekend and I want some grand champion dick," she slowly said while swiping her tongue across my earlobe.

That shit had a nigga ready to explode on himself.

"I got you, shawty," I assured as I licked my lips.

"Don't let me down," she said before walking back towards her apartment, ass jiggling along the way.

"Damn," was all I could say as I shook my head.

I waited outside a little while longer so Dre could see me as soon as he pulled up. Soon as I was about to call him to see where he was at, I could hear his loud music blasting up the street. When I lifted my head, it was him driving crazy as hell, and he was headed my way. Today he was driving a '92 ocean-blue Chevy Caprice with 24-inch rims, dark tint, and bull horn attached to the bottom of the hood. I hopped in on the passenger side and noticed that the interior was coconut cream with white leather seats, with Caprice written on the seats. It smelled like a pound of weed was in the air. Dre had that new Meek Mill "Dream Chaser 4" blasting from the speaker.

"Wassup, bruh!" Dre yelled as he nodded his head to the music.

"Nun much, nigga. I just wanted to cash my check," I informed him.

"Man! Whenever you ready to make some real money, come holla at me."

"Nall, I'm good. I can't go back to that lifestyle."

"Whatever you say, bruh. I wish you the best of luck with them small ass checks you working for. But what up with you and Trina though? She still holding back on your ass?"

"Hell yeah, bruh. She still ain't playing fair, but it's cool though, because I been bonding with Faith, and at the end of the day, that's all that matters. I was amazed at how Albany had really changed since the last time I was out.

"So how far your sister stay?" I inquired.

"She doesn't stay far. She lives over there in Double Gate."

Anybody who stayed over there had some cash. On the way to his sister house, I leaned back and played on my phone and checked my Facebook messages. I hadn't been on Facebook for ten minutes when I was alerted that I had a message. I clicked on the message and a smile instantly began to spread across my face. A woman who was interested in my services hit me up asking for my prices. I gladly sent her my prices and decided to only charge fifty for an hour session. The session was included with a light workout, three days out the week. The woman told me the best time to meet her was Wednesday evening, and I told her that was fine with me. I was so busy talking to my new client that I didn't even know that we had made it to Dre's sister house until we pulled up in her driveway. Dre's sister house was on point, and I promised myself that as soon as I got my money looking right, I was going to get something just as nice. The grass was bright green, and the bushes were trimmed. She lived in a two-story home with a two-car garage. I could see the red car he picked me up in when I first got out of prison.

Dre parked the car, jumped out, and headed to the front door.

I was just about to head inside when my phone began to ring.

"Hello," I said as I glimpsed down at my screen.

"May I speak to Elijah Champion?" the woman asked.

"This him."

"This is Faith's school. I was calling to see if you could come and pick Faith up; she passed out not to long ago. Right now, she is in the nurse's office laying down."

My heart dropped.

"I will be there," I managed to choke out.

I didn't bother by going inside Dre's sister house. Instead, I called him on the phone and told him what had happened. A few minutes later, he was back in the car, and Dre swerved in and out of traffic as we headed to Faith's school.

CHAMP

On our way to Faith's school, my heart was pumping a mile a minute. All I could think about was my baby girl. I just prayed that everything was okay with her. I bit down on the inside of my lips because my nerves were through the roof. As soon as I got the call from the school, I immediately hit Trina up to let her know what was up. I told her that Dre was dropping me off at the school and asked if I could catch a ride back with her. She messaged me back and told me that the school had already called and she was on the way as well.

As Dre pulled up at the school, I told him to drop me off at the front door. I hopped out and headed inside the building where I was met with some cold ass air. I shivered just a little before I took a look around the big ass school, not really knowing where the fuck I was going. I had never been to Faith's school before, so I had no clue where the front office was even located at. The inside of Faith's school looked as if I had stepped into another dimension. The carpet looked expensive as hell, and the walls were filled with expensive plaques of the staff that I assumed worked there.

Faith was enrolled in a Christian-based school called Sherwood. Sherwood was one of the top schools that had the highest academy rate in the country. Most of the students that attended this school later became doctors, lawyers, and politicians. This was Faith's first year in this program, and Trina was all in for Faith to have the best education that she could receive. A few minutes later of looking around, I finally came to a big wooden door that said 'Office' in big bold letters. I was just about to open the door when Trina stepped out with a tall, skinny, black woman with salt and pepper hair. The lady had on an all-black dress with thick glasses dangling from her neck.

Trina looked up at me as if she was shocked to see me there.

"You got here quick as hell," Trina commented.

"You know Dre drive crazy as hell."

"Mrs. Franklin, this is Faith's father," Trina introduced us.

I extended my hand because I didn't want to appear rude, but all I truly wanted to know was how my baby was doing.

"Is Faith okay?" I asked as I wiped the sweat from my face.

"Yeah, she is okay; she just got too hot," Mrs. Frankly said, giving Trina a paper to sign.

"Do' y'all plan on taking Faith home today?"

"Yes, ma'am," Trina said as she finished signing the form.

I just stood there and watched as Trina handled all that. I was just happy that Faith was okay. After Trina and Mrs. Franklin were done talking, Mrs. Franklin stepped inside the office and a second later, I heard the intercom telling Faith Anderson to report to the main office.

"Thanks for coming," Trina stated as she and I took a seat next to one another.

"When it comes to Faith, I will always be here," I assured her.

I could smell Trina's perfume as I leaned closer to her.

"I'm glad that you and her are bonding; just don't go back to your old ways, Champ, because that will only break her heart."

"Trina, you ain't never got to worry about that."

I already knew Trina was still stuck in the past. I mean, she knew how I used to be; how reckless I was, and how I didn't give a fuck about anything. Right before I went off to prison, I didn't care about anything but my damn self. I could understand Trina's concern and worries. Things were going to be totally different now. There was no way I could do anything to break my baby girl's heart.

"Okay, Champ," she responded slowly as she touched my hands. Her touch did something to a nigga. My heartbeat began to increase as she and I stared into each other's eyes. Our faces were moving closer to each other, and I could feel her warm breath on my face.

The moment was ruined when Trina's phone began to ring. The spell was broken, and I didn't know if I was happy or pissed off about the shit. She answered the call and told whomever what was going on with Faith. I just sat there trying to find something to do so I could take my mind off Trina and I almost kissing. When I lifted my head up, I noticed my angel coming around the corner. When our eyes connected, she took off running towards me.

"Daddy!" Faith called out loudly.

I opened my arms and embraced her in a big hug so she would know that things were going to be okay. When I turned around and faced Trina, she looked at me as if she had just sucked on a sour lemon.

"Everything good?" I asked as I grabbed Faith's book bag and put it on my shoulder.

"Yeah, so far ... I guess," she said as she shrugged her shoulder.

"Faith, are you okay?" Trina asked as she turned her head from me and gave her attention to Faith.

Trina was always the type of woman who kept her feelings to herself. She always told me when other people knew what you truly felt inside, they could easily use that shit to hurt you. Within a few minutes, we were pulling up at Trina's apartment. The whole ride home, Trina didn't say anything to me, but she kept her face balled up like she was pissed off about some shit. When I glanced over at her one last time, she quickly looked away from me.

Faith had dozed off in the back seat, so I already knew I was going to have to carry her because there was no way she was going to walk up the stairs half sleep. I was just about to put Faith in my arms when Trina told me that I better wake her up and let her walk in the house herself. As I picked my daughter up, I understood why Trina told me to wake her up. My little princess was heavy, but it wasn't a big deal. After I had carried Faith in the house and put her in bed, I headed out the door and noticed that Trina was still outside gathering her school books. I waited around the front door because I wanted to know what was up with Trina and why she had that stank ass look all over her face.

"Excuse me," she uttered as she tried moving me out the doorway.

I didn't dare move which I knew pissed her off.

"Champ, I'm not in the mood to play right now."

This time, she pushed me vivaciously which made me jerk back a little because I wasn't even expecting it.

I grabbed her arm and looked deep into her eyes.

"Trina, what in the hell wrong with you?" I demanded.

"Champ, let me go!" she yelled as she tried to snatch away from me, but my grip was tight and firm. She wasn't about to go anywhere until she told a nigga something.

"Okay, damn," she broke down.

"Let it all out," I said, closing the front door behind her.

We took a seat on the couch where we had attempted our sexual encounter. Damn, I don't know why Trina was playing games with a nigga, but I wasn't going to force myself on her like that.

"What's wrong with you, shawty?"

She looked at me crazy like she wanted to smack a nigga.

"I mean, what's wrong, Trina," I corrected myself.

"Tyrone canceled out on me again," she confessed.

"Mann, you over here Justin Timberlake about a nigga?" I said, trying to lighten up the mood, but I could tell she was still upset.

"Whatever," she shot back.

"Look, I apologize. Tell me the issue with you and lil' buddy."

She stopped and stared at me as if she was debating if she should tell me anything. She inhaled then exhaled before she began explaining her relationship with Tyrone.

"Tyrone and I been together for four years. I feel like he's the only one for me, but he's married. He's been telling me that he's going to leave his wife, but he ain't made a move yet. He a big-time lawyer with major paper."

She continued to talk as I listened to her, and when she asked for my advice, you know a nigga was straight up real with her. I told her that fucking around with married men was something she didn't want to get herself involved in. But she felt she was in too deep to pull out now. When she told me that he had been helping her out with her bills, etcetera, I just looked away from her because who was I to judge her for her decisions.

Trina wiped her eyes and began to ask me personal questions that had a nigga trying to figure out what was actually running through her mind.

"So, how you and ole girl doing?" she asked.

"Who you talking about?

Trina shook her head in disbelief.

"Roshika."

I just smirked and half laughed as I tried brushing her off, but Trina was standing over me with her hands on her hips.

 "Champ, I know you too well. You can't get nothing pass me."

"Well, you should already know she ain't nothing but a quick nut, that's it, since you know me so well."

"You better be careful," Trina warned me playfully as she pushed my head back.

"Nall, you the one who better be careful. That man wife finds out about you, you already know it's going to be trouble," I joked, as I tried to sound like Bernie Mac.

We both burst out laughing.

"She don't want to see me," Trina boasted.

I smirked at her comment.

Trina was the type of chick that was always into her education, but Trina was raised around her cousins and uncles who roughed her up, so she was always fighting. I never had to worry about Trina protecting herself, because I knew she could handle herself if needed. It was some men that wasn't on their game, and Trina could seriously knock there asses out. I remember when I first saw her drag a female.

It was a Thursday night, and the state fair had just hit Albany. My paper was on point, so I was shining like no other. I had rented a fly ass whip to take to the special event. It was me, Trina, and some of her little cousins that was riding along with us. The night was perfect; the weather wasn't too hot or cold. I was fresh from head to toe and had bitches eyeing me like they wanted to get a taste of me. I was rocking a crisp white t-shirt, blue Polo denim jeans, cocaine white Air Forces with a custom fitted cap that read "Champ," and my favorite dark tinted shades followed by a gold chain that all had the bitches wanting to get my number.

Trina was on point as well. She was killing the game with her black Armani overall short set, white wife beater for her undershirt, a pair of black half boots, and her Louis Vuitton shades to match. We strolled through the major entrance with no issues and saw a few people we knew. We spoke and chatted with some before we waved goodbye. When we finally made it through the line, we rode on a few rides just before Trina dragged me to this concession stand and pointed to a bear that she had to have. This girl almost spent half her damn money trying to toss the ball at the three bottles that were standing up on a wooden table. When she finally won the bear of her choice, her face lit up like she was a Christmas tree. Things were going smoothly until we made our way to the funnel cake stand.

"Hey, Champ," a female voice called out my name. Trina and I both turned around at the same time. When I noticed it was Yolanda, which was a girl I was fucking around with off and on, I tried to just speak and prayed that nothing popped off.

"Damn, Champ, it's like that?" Yolanda asked.

I bit the bottom of my lip, turning back around like I didn't even hear her ass. But Yolanda was adamant that she was going to get my attention. I was glad when Trina was next up in line to order her funnel cake.

"Nall, it ain't like that but, I—" I was cut off really quick by Trina who was staring at me and Yolanda to figure out who we were talking to.

"Champ, who this bitch is!" Trina yelled, standing between us.

"Oh, hell nall. Who the fuck you calling a bitch? I got your bitch!" Yolanda yelled back.

I don't know why Yolanda decided she was going to fuss with Trina. Yolanda stepped to Trina and was just about to say some more shit, but Trina quickly punched her in the mouth. It caught her off guard because she stumbled just a little. Trina was landing punches left and right, and Yolanda didn't have a chance to even defend herself. I quickly broke that shit up because I felt bad as hell that Yolanda had gotten her ass beat over me. But Yolanda already knew I had a girl, so when she saw Trina, she should have just left me alone. All the other chicks I was fucking around with knew not to say shit to me when I was with Trina, because Trina didn't play. She was ready to body any bitch over me. The whole night, Trina gave me hell. That was one ass whooping that sent a message to all my other side chicks not to speak to me.

As I stared at Trina, I shook my head at her expression.

"Yeah, I know you can handle yourself, but be careful because I don't want to fuck lil' buddy up about you," I said, giving her that serious look.

"Look at you," Trina joked.

"Well, I guess it's just going to be you, me, and Faith tonight."

"Yeah, I guess it will then." I grinned.

Since I had been out of prison, this was going to be the very first night that she and I were going to be staying under the same roof. Normally her ass was out with her boyfriend while I was home watching Faith.

I told myself if the time was right, I was going to see if Trina was down to fuck a nigga, but the fact that Trina wasn't showing me any play I decided to not even try her tonight.

I licked my lips as I got a good view of Trina's sexy ass as she stood up and headed towards her bedroom. I stared at the ceiling as I began to have thoughts of just how much I missed being with Trina. I couldn't help but wonder what would have happened between her and I if I never would have gotten locked up. The memories we shared were unbelievable, and the more I thought of them, the more I wanted to devour her. I truly wanted us to be a family, but I didn't know if Trina was even thinking about settling down with me right now. My thoughts were driving me crazy, and there was nothing I could really do to make them stop. I stood up off the couch, stretched, and found myself walking towards Trina's room. I was just about to knock on her door when it swung open. She looked shocked to see me but her eyes never left mine.

Trina could read me like a book, so she already knew what was up. As our lips connected, electricity began to shoot up and down my body. I slid my tongue into Trina's mouth as she wrapped her arms around my neck and pulled me into her room. This was my first time even stepping in her room, so I knew that today was going to be the day that Trina finally broke me off some of her kitty Kat. When our faces detached, Trina took it upon herself and began to strip me naked. Only thing Trina had on was a long gray t-shirt and some sweatpants that she removed in less than a second.

Her chocolate colored skin was oiled up, and her skin was smooth and soft. I took her breasts in my mouth and gently began to suck each one of her nipples as she moaned out my name. She smelled so good, and all I wanted to do was lick and suck her body in places that I hadn't seen in years. She laid down on the bed as I roamed my hands up and down her naked body. When I slid my finger into her pussy, she was dripping wet. I dropped down on my knees and slid open her pussy lips and began to get to work, sucking and licking on her clit while I slid my two fingers in and out of her pussy.

Trina continued to moan and cry out my name as my tongue dipped in and out of her wet pussy. The more my tongue dipped in and out of her pussy, the more her nails were dug into my back. I didn't stop until her legs started shaking.

"Champpppp…" she cried out.

I lifted my head up as I kissed her all the way back up to her neck. I could feel her hand stroking the tip of my ten-inch monster. Trina had that effect on a nigga that no other female could ever have. She knew exactly how to please me, and for that, she would always be my number one. When I slid my pole inside her, I swear I felt I had caught me a flight to outer space. She was super wet, tight, and warm inside.

"Damnnn," Trina moaned as she looked into my eyes.

I thrust in and out in a nice steady motion. I didn't want to nut too fast because I wanted to enjoy this pussy, and I wanted her to enjoy this dick. Every time a nigga thrust inside her, Trina tightened her pussy muscles up. Fucking around with Trina began to bring back old memories and feelings that I still had for her. She grabbed the back of my lower back and pushed me deeper into her.

"Champ!" Trina screamed as she stuck her nails in my back.

"Shitttt, fuck me harder," she encouraged me.

I thrust in harder and deeper as she wished.

"Champ, I'm about to cummmmmm!" Trina yelled out as she clasped me with a firm grip.

I flipped Trina over on her stomach and ran my hand up and down her tiger tattoo. Trina loved her ass some tigers, but I always preferred the lions of the jungle. I began kissing her sweaty back, and when I got to her big beautiful ass, I took both my hands and began caressing it. Trina arched her back and signaled for me to slide into her. Trina was looking sexy as hell with sweat dripping from her face. She blew a kiss at me, turned around, and placed her face in her pillow. As I slid my dick into her, she slowly began to throw her ass back on me. I kept my palms face down on her ass cheeks as I gave her some deep strokes.

"Shit!" Trina moaned out as she pushed her face farther down in the pillow.

I kept pounding her pussy because I knew I was hitting the spot that she loved the most. I put both hands around her small waist and shot out everything I had inside of me. She was still moving back and forth even though she had drained the soul out of me. When I slid out of her, my dick and stomach was wet with her juices.

"Damn, nigga," Trina said, flipping over on her back and brushing her hair out of her face.

"Champ," Trina gushed softly.

I turned to face her and pulled her down beside me. She laid her head on my chest and began to rub her hand up and down my chest.

"You know this wasn't supposed to have happened."

I smirked.

"I'm for real, Champ, I—" but I cut her off.

"I understand where we stand at. Right now, let's just enjoy the moment," I said as I played in her hair.

As much as I wanted to be in Trina's life, I still knew I had a lot of work to do to get myself all the way right. I already knew when the time came I was going to get my baby back. Within minutes, Trina was off to sleep. When I tried moving her off my chest, she grabbed me, but I gently laid her on her pillow. I slid off the bed, got up, put my clothes back on, and left out her room. As I turned around and stared back at Trina, I noticed that she had pulled the sheets over her head and she was sleeping so peacefully.

"One day I will have you back in my life," I whispered to myself as I closed the door behind me.

SASHA

Today was the day that I decided to go to the gym and work out. I wasn't overweight or anything like that; I just felt as if I had a little more stomach that I wanted to lose. To be honest, I really just wanted to get the hell out of the house for a while. I was tired of sitting home being lonely. I stood outside with Ashanti and Malcolm as we waited on the bus to pick them up for school. We all waved at Ryan as he hopped in his car and pulled out the driveway to head to work for the day. When the bus pulled up, I kissed both my kids on the forehead and told them to have a great day at school. I was just about to head into the house when I spotted my neighbor. I waved at Betty, who had been my neighbor for over five years. She was the only one in the neighborhood that I had bonded with throughout the five years that she had been living in the neighborhood.

After I cleaned up the house and showered, I began to get nervous as I thought about the personal trainer that I had so-called booked to help with my workouts. I mean, did I really even need to spend money on a damn personal trainer? I asked myself. After I had pulled my hair up in a ponytail, I decided to wear a pair of black leggings, a pink and black top that read "kick ass" in all bold letters, and a pair of pink and black Air Max to match. As I stared at myself in my mirror, I took a quick picture and saved it in my phone. After I was satisfied with my appearance, I headed to the living room where I heard something vibrating on the couch. I was not going to lie, I had been on edge since I had learned that Geno was alive. I mean, I didn't know where this nigga was at. I didn't even know if he knew where I lived.

As I neared the couch, I reached between the seat as I tried searching for the vibrating device. When I pulled out Ryan's phone, I was shocked because he always kept his phone on him. When I looked down and noticed that the name read "Anderson," my heart skipped a beat. I wanted to answer it, but I decided to just leave the shit alone and let it go straight to voicemail. I was just about to place the phone in my purse when it began to vibrate in my hand. I wanted to answer it, but my heart wouldn't even let me. Instead, I stuck the phone in my purse and headed out the door.

As opposed to heading straight to the gym for my appointment, I took a detour and headed towards Ryan's firm so I could drop off his phone. His phone began to vibrate yet again in my purse, which was really irritating the shit out of me. When I pulled up at a red light, I dug the phone out my purse to see who was calling, and yet again, it read Anderson. I couldn't wrap my mind around who the fuck Anderson was. I mean, it has to be business related, I told myself.

When the light turned green, I bit the bottom of my lip as the conversation with Sweet Pea about the married man that she was dealing began to invade my brain. This shit was driving me up the wall because what if Ryan was out fucking around on me. What would I do? Would I leave or would I stay? As I neared Ryan's law firm, I noticed a sign that I had never seen before which read "Truth." I inhaled then exhaled as I tried to clear my mind of all the negative energy that I was feeling inside. I turned on the radio to try to take my mind off things, but that shit only made it worse. When Keyshia Cole's voice started blasting through the speakers, I quickly turned that shit off. Keyshia was only going to get me in my feelings more deeply than I wanted to.

When I finally pulled up at Ryan's law firm, I had to ride around his parking lot twice before I found a damn parking space. I shook my head as I slid on my Gucci shades and exited my car. It had been over seven months since I'd last come to my husband's job. The last time I came, I had surprised him with lunch. I only came to his office when I truly had to, and lately, I had no reason to pop up.

When I made it through the door, the scent of French fries hit my nostrils. As I neared the reception desk, I noticed that the office had been redecorated. The office was tastefully decorated in a southern home-style setting. There were two leather couches sitting parallel from each other, and a glass table with different legal magazines were arranged neatly on the table. There was tan carpet that ran throughout the whole office, and there also was a few plants that were sitting in the windows to get sunlight. Whoever had decorated the office had done a good ass job.

Ryan's secretary was sitting behind her desk, but as I approached her, I immediately recognized that she was new. His last secretary was a woman name Yasmen and she always kept a smile on her face. This new girl looked awfully young and looked like she was fresh out of college.

"May I help you?" the secretary asked as she flipped her hair to the side with her free hand.

"Will you page Ryan, please," I politely requested, as I placed my purse on the counter to remove his phone from my bag.

"Do you have an appointment with him?" the secretary asked, taking a quick glimpse over some forms that she had clipped on her clipboard that was laying on her desk.

I smirked before I replied, "I don't need an appointment."

Since I didn't know her, I took my shades off from over my eyes so she could get a good look at me. I was pretty sure that she had seen my pictures inside Ryan's office and knew exactly who I was.

"Well, without an appointment, you won't be able to see him," the secretary said with a half fake smile as she grabbed the phone and began to munch on her French fries.

I promise you it took everything for me to keep my composure because I swear I was a few minutes away from dragging this young bitch.

"Um, excuse me."

I took a deep breath. She looked up and gave me the look like why the hell was I still there. I clenched my teeth because I didn't want to get out of character this morning messing with a young hoe.

"You must can't understand English or something. If you ain't got no appointment you ain't going to see him," she spoke with a nasty attitude.

I really couldn't take it anymore; this little bitch had blown my last nerve.

"Bitch, you got me all the way fucked up!" I yelled.

The classy woman had gone out the window, and I was ready to go back to them project days and beat a bitch's ass to the pavement.

I snatched my purse up off the counter and headed towards my husband's office.

"I got your bitch!" she yelled back. This bitch had me so damn mad and frustrated that I could barely even think logically. When I approached Ryan's office, I noticed that his door was closed. I started to knock but decided against it. Instead, I twisted the knob and stepped inside. He was chatting on the phone and appeared to be having a deep conversation. As soon as he saw me step into his office, he quickly told the person on the line that he would talk with them later.

"Sasha, is everything okay?" Ryan asked as he began to fix his clothes.

"That little black bitch out there has pissed me the fuck off," I spat as I pointed towards the lobby.

Right when I was just about to finish my statement, her and two police officers were coming through the door.

"There she goes, officers," the secretary told the police.

Ryan reacted fast as hell as he jumped between me and the police officers.

"Wait a minute, what's going on here?" he questioned as he put his hands up.

Ryan looked at me and then to the little bitch that he had so called hired to replace Yasmin.

"This woman just bum rushed me at the front desk and came back to your office without an appointment," the secretary said.

This bitch was actually looking like she had saved the damn day. She just didn't know that after today, her ass wasn't going to even have a job.

"This is my wife," Ryan said sternly.

When Ryan said that shit, it looked like all the air inside her had deflated. I just stood there with the same expression on my face, trying to see why this bitch had called the police.

"Officers, I greatly apologize about this misunderstanding," Ryan told them professionally as he showed them to the door. I took that time and took a seat on his leather couch as I thought about how that bitch looked when she found out that I was Ryan's wife. As my mind began to spin, I felt in my soul that something wasn't right about that bitch. I stood up because I was beginning to get agitated, so I headed over to where he had his books stacked up on the bookshelf and ran my hands across him. Ryan's office was neat and clean and looked like any other lawyer's office, but something was out of place; something was missing. There were no pictures of me or his family nowhere in his office. The only thing he had on his desk was his laptop, a name plate, rubber band container, and a telephone. I was just about to get in my feelings when Ryan stepped back into his office.

I didn't hesitate to step to his ass either.

"Sasha! What are you doing here?" he asked with attitude. He must have known he had said the wrong shit to me before he took a step back.

Just hearing him ask me some shit like that felt as if he had punched me in my gut.

"What the fuck you mean what I'm doing here?" I barked at him. I stepped closer to his ass as I pointed my finger in his face.

"I didn't mean it like that. I just wasn't expecting you." Ryan tried consoling me with a softer tone, but it was too late; I was pissed the fuck off."

"Whatever," I snapped as I walked out the door.

He grabbed me by my arm, but I snatched away from him and gave him a sinister look.

"Sasha, what's up with you?"

"You need to fire that disrespectful bitch," I told him angrily before reaching into my purse and throwing his phone at him.

As I walked back towards the lobby so I could dip out, I noticed the little bitch was sitting there sitting at the front desk talking on the phone to somebody. Our eyes locked but no words were exchanged.

When I got back to the parking lot, I glanced at my watch and noticed that I was running late for my appointment. I was a little pissed off because I wasn't expecting to run into a new secretary who had no class and didn't know how to talk to people. I hopped in my car and jetted off towards Dawson Road. As I swerved throughout traffic, all I could think about was dragging that hoe for disrespecting me. The fact that Ryan had the nerve to ask me why I was at his job in the first place, really had me pissed the fuck off. Since when did I need an appointment to see my own damn husband? That nigga had me fucked all the way up. I had been calm all these years, but I was ready to fuck somebody up.

"Sasha, you need to calm down," I tried to assure myself, but the other part of me said "Fuck that shit."

This nigga didn't even have none of our family pictures anywhere in his office, which was part of the reason why I wanted to drag his ass first. If he would have had some pictures up of his family, then she would have known exactly who I was, so I wasn't going to place all the blame on her. But that still didn't change the fact that she still was a rude bitch.

I was so caught up in my damn feelings that I was startled when I heard the police sirens behind me.

"Shit," I cried.

I couldn't help but panic as I looked out my rearview mirror as the officer walked up to my car. I hated police officers. I mean, they always made me nervous as hell when they were anywhere near me. There was no way police could be trusted these days, and I never wanted to end up at the wrong place or wrong time.

"How can I help you, officer?" I asked innocently and calmly as I could.

The officer was a slim, tall white male, with salt and pepper hair on his head and face, a long narrow nose, and a scent so awful that I wanted to throw up when he opened his mouth.

"Ma'am, you was speeding; you was going fifty miles per hours in a thirty-mile per hour area," he explained as he removed his shades from his face.

"I honestly didn't realize that I was going that fast," I noted as I tried giving him a pitiful expression so he would let me go because I had just paid a speeding ticket less than six months ago.

"I need for you to hand me your license and registration."

I handed the officer what he asked for as I waited for him to give them back. I watched as he headed over to his cruiser, and I instantly began to say a silent prayer. My heart was pounding a mile a minute and my nerves were over the roof with worry. At this very moment, I wanted nothing then to head right back at Ryan's job, dragging him and that thot ass all up and down Albany's streets. This was the second time that I had come face to face with the law today, and it wasn't even five o'clock yet.

When I was younger and in the streets, I barely even saw the police, so I knew her bitch ass probably had set this shit up. She was lucky that I wasn't the same ratchet chick that I used to be twenty years ago. Where I was from, if you snitched or did some foul shit, you would be the first who was going to get fucked up. If you didn't die, you was going to wish you would have never opened your mouth.

When Ryan got his ass home tonight, he and I needed to sit down so we could talk about a lot of shit, because after today, he needed to find him another secretary because there was something about that bitch that just wasn't right. The second thing I wanted to talk to him about was why the fuck he didn't have any pictures of me or the kids in his office. I mean, I found that shit strange as hell. If I was married with kids, of course I would want to let people know when they stepped in my office that I was off the market and proud to be.

"Ma'am, here are your license and registration back," the officer said as he handed me back my information and a copy of my ticket. I placed them in my passenger seat and rolled up my window as I waited for the police officer to pull off first. When he had disappeared in traffic, I threw the clutch into gear and proceeded to my original destination.

CHAMP

I was so pissed off right now that I could barely even think straight. I had been here for the past hour waiting on my new client, who didn't even have the decency to call me to let me know she wasn't going to show up. I swear, when I did see her ass, I was going to let her know that if she wasn't serious about taking my class then she needed to let me know, because I had better shit to be doing then trying to work with her. When I glanced down at my watch and saw the time, I knew it was time for me to leave. I had already made up my mind that when I left, I was going to head back to Jerome's place because Trina had been acting all funny with me, and Faith had been asking me all these questions about Trina and I getting back together.

I didn't want to be the one to mislead my daughter, so I decided the best thing to do was stay low and stay away from them both. When Jerome told me earlier that day that he had found me a place to stay, I didn't hesitate to take him up on the offer. I had a little money saved up and felt like God was finally answering my prayers. I had gotten out the pen, found me a job, and was soon going to have my own place.

"Aye!" I shouted to Tonya who was sitting down behind the podium playing with her phone.

"If someone come looking for me, let them know I have dipped out!" I shouted as I grabbed my tote bag.

"Alright," she flirted.

"Aye!" she yelled out to me.

I turned around to see what she wanted.

"I'm not your secretary either," she joked.

"Damn, it's like that!" I shouted back to her.

"Champ, you know I got you," she said as she tried to play with her tongue to let me see her tongue ring.

My eyes roamed over her body until it stopped at her titties.

"Appreciate it," I said as I turned around, throwing up the deuces.

I had to get the fuck up out of there before Tonya got a nigga in trouble. Tonya was the type of chick that didn't mind expressing her sexual wild side. She was down for whatever, and if it had something to do with money, then she was definitely down to do whatever she had to do to get her Benjamin's. Money was her god, and no one could tell her differently.

Tonya was the true definition of a human blood sucker. When she got her palms on a nigga, she was going to suck his ass dry until he was gasping for air. Tonya was about five feet nine inches tall, light bright complexion, 165 pounds, hair was long down her back, deep dimples, with a gold bright bottom grill. She had perky B-cup breasts, and an ass that sat perfectly on her back. I tried my best to stay far away from her because I knew she came with a whole lot of drama.

When I stepped outside, it was still hot as hell. I almost broke a sweat as I threw my Nike bag across my shoulder and walked towards my car. Jerome had found me a nice whip so I could get around with. It wasn't nothing flashy, but it was better than walking or asking for a ride. I was driving a two toned '99 Crown Victoria with no air or heat. These past couple days, I went to the driver services to get my license because without them bitches, Jerome wouldn't even let a nigga get behind the wheel. When I had made it halfway to the car, my phone starting ringing.

"Hey, sexy," Roshika flirted.

"What's going on with you, Shika?" I asked as I unlocked my car door.

"You. Are you still coming over tonight?" she taunted me.

"Yeah, right now I'm about to head to Albany Management Property so I can view this apartment," I informed her.

"That's what up."

"As soon as I'm done, best believe I will come through."

After we had said our goodbyes to one another, I threw my phone in the passenger seat and slid my key in the ignition, but every time I turned the key, the car wouldn't start. I tried a few more times, but the car still did the same damn thing. I popped the rusty hood and checked to see what the fuck was going on with my car. I sighed with frustration as I jiggled the wires by the engine, and shook my head when I noticed that my radiator was leaking.

"Fuck," I said to myself. I grabbed the jug of water out of the trunk of my car and poured it into the right spot. I was just about to shut the hood of the car when I noticed a figure approaching me. At the moment, I couldn't really make out if it was a man or woman. I reached out to grab my crowbar but remembered I had left it in the car.

Damn, I normally always kept a weapon on me because you never knew when a nigga would get crazy and walk up on you. I was the type of nigga to bust a nigga's jaw and ask questions later.

"Excuse me," a woman's voice called out.

When I completely shut the hood of my car, our eyes locked on one another.

"You," I responded without even noticing I had said anything directly to her.

"You the woman from the movies? What are you doing here?" I asked her curiously.

Her whole demeanor changed and she looked like I had just slapped her across her face.

"I've been hearing this statement all damn day," she muttered as she looked at her clock on her phone.

"The girl at the desk told me that I could find you out here."

"For?"

"My name is Sasha. I was the one who wanted to hire you as my personal trainer," she informed me irritably.

Damn, it was a small world. Never did I ever think I would be meeting this woman again and here she stood.

"First off, you late."

She put her hands up in the air.

"Let me explain."

"No need to. The less I hear about your personal life, the less I have to deal with."

"Are you still going to be my personal trainer?" she asked politely.

I glanced at the sky as the sun beamed down on my face before I stared back at her as she awaited my answer. There was no way I could turn her down because I needed the money.

"Yes, I will be your personal trainer. But next time you need to be on time, and if something comes up and you can't make it, make sure you call the office and inform me."

"I'm so sorry about that," she apologized.

I nodded my head.

When she pulled out her wallet and handed me a hundred-dollar bill, I looked at her like she was insane.

"Look, this is for wasting your time. This is your business, and I was wrong for not calling to let you know I was going to be late."

I took her hundred-dollar bill and deducted it for her membership for that month.

She and I came up with a time that both of us agreed on before we shook hands and I hopped in my car and sped off into traffic.

****

LATER THAT NIGHT

Knock, Knock!

The door slowly came open as Roshika appeared from behind. Her perfume invaded my nostrils as she smiled at me. She was looking sexy as hell, sporting a sexy black silk lace bra and a black silk lace thong. I licked my lips as I stepped insider her place. Roshika had outdone herself this time. She had her lights dimmed with scented candles that were lit around the living room.

"Mmmm, I been waiting on you all day," Roshika admitted seductively as she pulled me towards her.

When our lips touched, I swear that shit woke my dick up.

"I see someone else been craving me to," Roshika bragged as she slid her hands down my pants and caressed my dick.

As I stared into her eyes, I couldn't help but see the lust staring back at me. I was just about to say something but she gently placed her finger over my lips to silence me. She grabbed me by my hand as we walked towards the kitchen. After we had made it into the kitchen, I noticed a small birthday cake with her name written on it in red letters. She kissed me on my lips before telling me to have a seat. I smiled as I did as I was commanded. I swear Roshika always had some shit up her sleeve. She was big on role playing, and I was ready to see exactly what she had in mind for tonight. I waited as she connected her phone to her boom box that was sitting on the kitchen table by the cake. When Rihanna's "Sex With Me" came on over the speaker, I already knew she was about to put it on me.

Roshika loved her some damn Rihanna. When she turned her attention back to me, I noticed a devilish smile on her face. I groaned as she unsnapped her bra, slid off her black thong, and let them drop to the floor. She stepped between my legs, bent down, and slid her tongue into my mouth. Our tongues danced together for the longest time before she pulled away and pulled my shirt over my head. After my shirt was in the pile next to her clothes, she began to kiss on each tattoo that was on my neck all the way to my stomach.

I brushed her long hair out my face as she began to unfasten my belt and pull down my boxers and pants. She stood back up as I placed my arms around her hips and began to kiss and lick on her stomach, her soft moans made my dick harder by the second. She pulled away a few moments later, headed towards the counter, and pulled out a butcher knife. A nigga's heart stopped and she must have seen the confusion on my face.

She laughed before saying, "This ain't that type of party, relax."

I nodded my head as I watched to see just what Roshika was up to. The fact was that I had been locked up for so many years and had heard so many stories about these crazy ass women, that I wasn't about to trust no bitch with my life. Watching the ID channel all the damn time while locked up damn sure didn't help because I swear some people had some sick ass thoughts. I watched as she used the knife to cut a slice of cake. As she held the sliced cake in her hand, she gestured for me to open my mouth wide. The cake was sweet and moist as I ate each piece she placed in my mouth. When she placed some cake into her mouth and placed her lips on mine, I swear this bitch drove me wild. After the slice was demolished, she then began to rub the icing from the rest of the cake over my rock-hard manhood.

I moaned as she got down on her knees and began to suck all the icing off my dick. I pushed her head up and down aggressively, making sure she didn't miss any of the icing. She smiled as she pulled away from me briefly, pushed my legs apart, and began to stroke my pole up while applying a little salvia. I was at the edge of my seat as she placed her mouth back on my dick and made it disappear into her mouth.

"Shitttt," I groaned out.

I swear this bitch was sucking the very life out of me. I pulled her up off her knees as she hopped on top of my dick. I licked and sucked on each of her perky nipples as she slid my dick into her. She rotated her hips and I held on to her ass as she began to fuck me.

"Shit, Champ!" Roshika screamed as she wrapped her hands around my neck.

She tilted her head back and planted her pals on my chest, as she began to slow grind on my dick. I could feel her juices wetting me up as she popped her pussy on a nigga. I was so into getting fucked that I didn't even hear her phone ring. After she had disconnected the call, she looked down at me and placed a kiss on my lips.

"I got a surprise for you, daddy," she whispered in my ear before she slid off my dick and headed to her front door. I rubbed my hands together as I began to imagine what the surprise was going to be. I was always down to have some more fun. When the door swung open, my eyes had to do a double take. I wasn't expecting to see Yolanda.

SASHA

"What the fuck you mean you ain't going to fire her!" I yelled at the top of my lungs at Ryan.

I was so pissed off at his ass that I had locked my damn self in the bathroom so I wouldn't do something to hurt him.

"Sasha, you are overreacting about nothing," he tried reassuring me.

He kept banging on the bathroom door, but I refused to open it.

"What you mean I'm overreacting!" I yelled again before I opened the bathroom door and pushed past him.

"The dumb bitch called the law on me," I said furiously as I shoved him with all my force.

He took a seat on the bed with his face in his palms. He lifted his head up as he stared at me as if he was trying to find the right words to say.

"Sasha, why you doing this?" Ryan asked calmly.

I wasn't in the mood to hear all this shit or answer his dumb ass questions.

"So, I'm the one with the problem?" I asked furiously.

I nodded my head as I eyed him in anger.

"Okay, cool. How about you leave me the fuck alone and go with your little bitch."

Ryan stood up as he tried to approach me, but I held my hands up to let him know not to touch me. I was fed up and I didn't want him putting his nasty hands on me.

"Sasha, you the only woman I love. I don't know what's wrong with you. You been acting strange lately."

I didn't bother by telling him I loved him back; instead, I gazed at him with a blank stare.

"I have to head to work. We will talk about this later," Ryan assured me.

I didn't respond. I just let him walk right out the door, not bothering to run after him to try to make him understand my pain.

For the past couple of days, Ryan and I had been going back and forth fussing with one another. I was far from crazy, but lately, my intuition was telling me that Ryan was up to something, but I had no clue at this moment exactly what it was. I flopped down on the bed as I began replaying all the shit that Ryan had done throughout the years. All the weekend trips were probably all lies. For all I knew, he probably had another family somewhere else. My thoughts were interrupted when I heard a knock on our bedroom door. When I saw Ashanti and the expression on her face, I quickly asked her if she was okay. Never had I ever let Ashanti or Malcolm witness me fussing with Ryan or crying. Over the past few years, I had kept my feelings bottled up and felt it was best to stay on my best behavior around the kids.

"Ma," Ashanti gasped out.

I could see the pain on her face. I gestured for her to come closer to me as I embraced her in a hug.

"What's wrong, baby?"

"Are you and daddy going to get a divorce?" she asked innocently.

I noticed the tears that were falling from her eyes, and I quickly wiped them away.

"No, baby, me and daddy are okay. Don't be worrying your pretty little head about us," I assured her.

"Now go finish getting ready for school."

I had been having so many crazy thoughts going through my mind that I could barely think straight. I hated the fact that Ashanti had just witnessed Ryan and I fussing. Never did I ever want to worry any of my kids, because I was once a kid. I remembered the effect that divorce had on kids. When my dad divorced my mom, it greatly affected me and I didn't want the same to happen to my kids. But at the same time, I wasn't about to sit around and allow a nigga to make a fool of me. I didn't care if he was my husband.

While Ashanti was getting ready for school, I decided to clean up my room because it needed it. I was hoping that maybe if I kept my mind busy I wouldn't have to keep stressing. Today, I was supposed to have gone to see my personal trainer, but he canceled because the weather was supposed to get bad. In the back of my mind, I was still shocked that the man who had practically saved my life was actually the man who was going to help me get my body back fit.

"What a small world," I said to myself as I began to fold up my clothes and put them away.

When I glanced at the clock, I noticed that it was time for Ashanti and Malcolm to head to school. I called out their names loudly, and they both came running down the stairs with their book bags over their shoulder.

Within an hour, I was pulling back up in my driveway. I sighed as I stepped out my car, grabbed my purse, and proceeded to my front door. Right before I inserted my key, I noticed one of my flower pots was cracked.

"Damn squirrel," I said to myself.

When I entered my house, I noticed a shadow which sent chills down my spine. I was just about to dip the fuck out when the figure ran towards me and snatched my ass up.

"I told you, bitch, I would find you," the stranger spat as he removed the ski mask from his face.

"Geno," I uttered.

He had a tight grip on my neck and I could barely breath.

I gasped for air but it didn't do any good. I closed my eyes as I tried to say a silent prayer.

"You have cost me a lot of money," he muttered, throwing me to the floor.

I thanked the man above as air finally reached my airway. I tried making a run for it, but Geno wasn't having any of that.

Wack!

I groaned in pain as he kicked me in the stomach.

"Help!" I tried screaming. I knew I was about to die.

"Bitch, ain't nobody going to help you." He grabbed me by my neck and kneeled down as he stared into my eyes.

"I'm going to kill you." He wrapped his massive hands around my neck and began to squeeze with all his might. I was fighting the best way I knew how, but he was too damn strong. I saw my life flash right before my eyes. The room started spinning and I felt as if I wasn't even on Earth any longer as I began to float towards the clouds.

"Ma, Ma, Ma."

When I opened my eyes, I saw Ashanti standing over me shaking me as hard as she could.

"Ma, are you okay?" Ashanti asked.

The first thing I did was touch my neck. It was all a dream. I grabbed Ashanti and gave her a tight hug. After cooking dinner for the kids to eat when they got home I had flipped on the T.V only to watch for no more than an hour because I knew the kids was going to be getting home soon. I must had dozed off by accident on the living room couch. I was relieved that everything that I had just experienced was only a nightmare.

CHAMP

I was heading to the gym today. This was going to officially be the first day that I trained with Sasha. I was still tripping at the fact my trainee was the same woman from the movies. Now that shit was kind of crazy. Then on top of that, seeing Yolanda the other night at Roshika's house ... Damn, I still couldn't twist my whole head around that shit. Yolanda didn't even look like she aged one bit. She told me she had just gotten out of a bad divorce with some crazy ass dude and was now a mother to a little boy. Just thinking about her brought back a lot of memories. I simply pushed those thoughts to the back of my head for the time being.

Walking inside Tony's Gym, Tonya's loud perfume attacked my nose as soon as I stepped across the threshold. Tonya was doing her usual talking on the phone and chewing her favorite gum. She was looking sexy as hell with her hair pulled back in a high ponytail with her fitted workout clothes on. She had her eyebrows arched to perfection and her makeup was applied just right. As I walked past her, I threw up my hand which caught her attention. In the back of my mind, I knew how she was sizing me up that she was down for some bullshit today.

"Heyyyyy ... Champ..." she flirted as she put more emphasis on my name. Whoever was on the phone must not have been talking about shit, because she quickly ended the call and turned her attention towards me.

"Wassup, Tee..." I said, leaning on the counter.

I grabbed a sour worm out her bag and put one in my mouth as I stared at her.

"You are so damn fine," she flirted as she snatched the bag back.

"Has my client made it here yet?"

"Yeah, she in the bathroom," Tonya replied as she licked her lips.

I just shook my head because I was not about to play myself out of pocket. I already had to figure out what I was going to do about Yolanda. When Trina found out that Yolanda had resurfaced, I knew she was going to give me hell. Even though Trina and I weren't together, that still wasn't going to stop her from making them slick comments about me trying to talk back with Yolanda. I mean, Yolanda had taken an ass whooping back in the day for me, so I was shocked when she seemed interested in catching up with me.

"Okay, cool," I commented as I hit the top of the counter and headed out to the floor to decide what my client and I were going to do first.

When I turned around, Sasha was standing behind me with her Nike gym bag at her feet. We didn't exchange words right away. I just nodded my head as I acknowledged her. She was dressed in a pair of black leggings, a white tank top, and a pair of grey Air Max. She had her hair pulled back in a neat ponytail and she had her lips glossed up with lip-gloss. I gestured for her to give me a second for me to change out of my regular clothes to my work-out clothes.

I stepped in the restroom and decided to put on my black Jordan shorts, and white T-shirt with the number 12 and a picture of a man jumping. I folded my other clothes in my bag as I took a look at myself in the mirror. I was looking sexy as hell as I flashed a smile that always seemed to make a bitch melt. When I stepped out the bathroom, I walked over to where Sasha was waiting for me.

"You ready?" I asked clapping my hands together to get her attention.

"I guess," she said half smiling.

I would have been lying if I said Sasha wasn't attractive, but what really had a nigga amazed with her was that she looked so innocent. As I got closer to her, I noticed that she had some flawless skin with no blemishes, acne, or wrinkles. My mother always told me that when you caught a woman who was flawless in the face, that only meant one thing: she probably didn't have a hard life.

"Before we begin, I want to introduce myself. My name is Champ," I said as I extended my hand out.

"My name is Sasha," the woman said as she touched my hand.

As our hands touched, sparks shot throughout my body. I thought I was tripping at first, but I knew deep down inside that I wasn't.

"I'm sorry about not showing up on time the other day," Sasha apologized.

"Don't worry about all that; it's in the past," I assured her as I grabbed our bags off the floor.

When I told Tonya to put the bags into my locker, she had a smirk on her face, but she did what she was told it. I watched her as she turned around and headed in the back. Damn, I thought to myself as I watched her ass jiggle from side to side with each step she took. I turned my attention back to Sasha and told her to follow me. As we stood in the middle of the gym, I pointed around to all the different areas that were offered. There were five different sections which included weightlifting, a boxing ring, gymnasium mat, a place for the treadmills and other cardio exercises, and a daycare center. It was not packed today, which was a good thing. It was a good vibe in the air, and everyone seemed like they were enjoying their work out. Tonya had Kevin Gates' "Satellites" blasting out the wall speaker, which had a nigga ready to do some serious work.

"When was the last time you worked out?" I asked Sasha.

I wanted to know because to me, nothing was wrong with Sasha's body. She had a nice shape already. If I had to guess, I would have thought that she worked out every day.

"Uh ... it's been a while," she said, glancing at the ground.

"I used to walk a lot, but right now, I just want to lose a few pounds. I feel like I'm fat." She laughed as she put her white headband on.

"Walking is good for the heart," I stated, glancing at the wall clock.

"Well, first we're going to stretch so we won't cramp up later," I informed her as I started showing her some simple stretching positions.

After ten minutes of stretching, I told her to follow me outside so we could go to the track for a walk. I didn't want to do too much today; didn't want to scare her off. The only thing she and I did were walk about two miles around the track as we had light conversation with one another. I was curious to know exactly where her mind was at first. By me being incarcerated for nearly nine years, I felt it was important for everyone to know who they were dealing with at all times. At first, she didn't open up to me, but I was expecting that because she and I didn't know anything about each other.

As the time began to fly by, she began to give me small details about her life. The little bit that she did tell me, I was grateful to know. She told me that she was married to a lawyer and that she had two kids (one boy and one girl). I knew she was married before she told me, by the enormous wedding ring on her finger. Overall, Sasha was a down to Earth female. She kind of reminded me of Trina.

"Well, that's it for today," I said, wiping the sweat off my face.

"I guess it is...." she noted as she gulped down her bottle water.

"We will meet in two days, so get ready to put in some work!" I exclaimed.

After Sasha and I headed back into the building, I split up from her and headed into the locker room so I could change out of my work-out clothes. When I was about to put my combination in, I heard a phone going off. I knew it wasn't mine because I left my phone in the car. When I finally opened the locker, I noticed that it was Sasha's phone that was ringing. I quickly grabbed her bag and went back in the lobby to give it to her. She was sitting on the bench with her head down with the towel around her head.

"Here you go. Oh yeah, your phone was ringing," I uttered as I handed her the bag.

"Thank you," she uttered as she retrieved her phone.

Right before she was about to check to see who was calling, it started ringing again. The expression on her face told me something was wrong. She grabbed her Nike bag then stormed out the door. When I turned around, Tonya was staring at me as if she wanted to rip my clothes off. I shook my head at her ass and then exited the gym.

SASHA

My heart was pounding and my nerves were through the roof. I was up here racing through traffic to get to my baby. I just couldn't believe that this was happening to me. Lord, let my baby be okay, I kept saying in my head. As I turned on 5th Street and then made a quick right on Madison and a left on Jefferson, I was relieved when the hospital came into view. I found the closest parking spot to the door before I threw the car into gear and hopped out. I ran through the sliding doors and headed straight to the front desk.

"I'm trying find my son's room," I blurted to the receptionist who was sitting at her desk as if she didn't have shit to do.

She looked up at me a with a stank expression. I swear if I wasn't so concerned about my son I would have punched the bitch in her face.

"Name?" she asked, chewing hard on whatever was in her mouth.

She was a plus-sized woman, with not much hair and hardly any edges. She looked like she'd been up for the past forty-eight hours because she had bags under her eyes.

"Malcolm Henderson," I said as I bit down on my lower lip. I tried my best to be patient.

I tapped my fingertips on the top of the counter as I waited for her to give me a room number or tell me something about my son.

"He is in room 325," she said, rolling her big bug eyes at me.

If you don't like your damn job, you should find another one. Don't be coming to work with that stank ass attitude, I thought to myself. I hated everything about hospitals, especially the smell, but I didn't give a shit about how much I hated being at a hospital right now; I was there because my son needed me. I grabbed my purse and pulled it over my shoulder as I headed towards the elevator and hopped on. The elevator didn't have that many people on it, which I was grateful for. I hit three and just stood back in the corner. I had my eyes closed the whole time as I said a silent prayer to myself. I didn't want anything to happen to my child, but I knew the man above was there holding my hand every step of the way. The sound of the elevator opening let me know I had arrived on my correct floor.

I quickly found room 325. When I entered, Sweet Pea and Ashanti were surrounding the bed.

When I got closer to the bed, my heart dropped to my feet. Seeing Malcolm lying in the bed like a sick patient only made tears began to fall down my face.

"Oh ... my God." I cuffed my mouth. "My baby ... my baby," I cried out emotionally.

"Ma!" Malcolm uttered as he tried sitting up in the bed.

I grabbed his hand then turned towards his doctor. Malcolm's doctor came in a few minutes after me and introduced himself. Doctor Wadley was a clean cut middle-aged gentleman, five feet six inches, dark complexion, salt and pepper wavy hair, slim, with a deep southern accent. He was very polite and well groomed.

"Doc, what's going on with my baby?" I asked, gripping Malcolm's hand tighter.

He read through Malcolm's chart before he cleared his throat.

"Well, ma'am." He took his glasses off, folding them and placing them in his pocket.

"Your son has a hole in his heart," he stated emotionally as he held up his test results.

"A hole?" Ashanti blurted out.

I gestured to Sweet Pea to take her down to the lobby so I could talk to the doctors in private.

"So, Doctor Wadley, when you say hole, what does that mean?" I carefully asked as I stared over at Malcolm who wore a blank expression on his face.

He set his clipboard down before he looked down at me.

"Well, Mrs. Henderson, to be honest—"

"'Please be honest," I cut in.

I had no time for his ass to be sugarcoating shit. He was talking extremely too slow to be trying to tell me the truth.

"Your son will be okay, but playing any kind of sport activities will be bad for his health."

When the doctor said that, I saw the disappointment on Malcolm's face. Malcolm was a very active child. He loved playing basketball and football.

"Right now, the hole is very large."

"Is there anything I can do?"

"Just keep him in a calm environment. I have seen incidents where the hole closes back up later down the line, so don't let this get you down," he assured me as he grabbed his clipboard.

"If you have any questions call this number."

He handed me a card and I placed it in my purse. I stepped towards Malcolm's bed and stared Malcolm in his eyes. I let him know everything was going to be okay. I closed my eyes and mumbled the 23 Psalms. My mother always told me when things seemed rough, the 23 Psalms was the best remedy for any solution. When I was done, I heard footsteps coming in the room. I turned around and there stood Ryan. When our eyes locked on one another, it's like all the anger I had for him went out the window. I immediately gave him a hug and kiss and informed him what was going on. We sat around the bed talking until Malcolm's nurse came to check Malcolm's vital signs.

" Is everything okay?" Ryan asked the nurse.

She nodded her head, then informed us that Malcolm was going to be released once we filled out some paperwork. Ryan helped Malcolm out the bed while I filled out the forms on his release. Once I was done I handed the forms back to the nurse.

"Daddy ... am I'm going to die?" Malcolm asked Ryan nervously.

"Son, you aren't going to die," Ryan responded passionately as he sat Malcolm in the leather colorful chair.

"Malcolm, everything is going to be okay. You can't kill Superman," Ryan said as he put his arms around his shoulder.

I just stood back enjoying that little moment of Ryan and Malcolm together. The nurse stepped back into the room with the discharge papers, and we headed straight to the elevator. As we headed down to the bottom floor, I stared at the two men in my life. That moment right there, I felt a sense of happiness. I grabbed Ryan by the hand and placed the other on Malcolm's shoulder. We all exited the elevator and ran into Sweet Pea and Ashanti who were eating some sour cream and onion chips. I knew that had to be Ashanti's idea because she loved them kind of chips. Even when I was pregnant with her, that was all I craved. She ran over and hugged Malcolm tightly. She loved her brother to death, and they always protected one another with all their might. Ryan pulled me toward him as Sweet Pea entertained the kids.

"Sasha, I'm about to run back to the office for a quick minute. I will be home in an hour," Ryan said as he kissed me on my lips.

"Okay, honey." Even though I was disappointed, I didn't let it show.

We all made it towards the parking lot and the kids waved Ryan goodbye.

"Are you sure you don't need me to help with anything?" Sweet Pea asked gently.

"No, honey. You head home; I got everything under control. Thanks for coming by to check on Malcolm."

"Anytime, love," Sweet Pea exclaimed before waving the kids bye, hopping in her car and pulling off.

.... SEVERAL HOURS LATER....

I'd been waiting on Ryan's lying ass for the last few hours to come home, and his ass still hadn't appeared. He messaged me earlier and told me he was wrapping things up. Shit, that was about three hours ago. When I tried to think with a clear head, he always disappointed me. I was so tired of being second to him. Something had to change fast. I grabbed my phone and called Sweet Pea. She didn't answer on the first ring so I tried calling her again.

"Mmmm..."

"Pea!" I yelled in the phone.

"Yeah," she grumbled.

"I need a favor.".

"Bitch, do you know what time it is?" Sweet Pea uttered into the phone.

"Never mind all that, I really need you."

"What you need?"

I informed her that I needed her to come over and watch the kids for me. When she told me that Rodney had her car, I told her I was willing to call an Uber for her so she would have a way over to my place.

I didn't have to wait no more than thirty minutes when a knock came at my door. I was glad as hell to see that Sweet Pea had finally made it. She was dressed in her bed clothes and looked tired as hell. She took a seat on my living room couch and asked me what in the hell I was up to. I didn't say a word but told her I needed to run a quick errand. There was no way I was about to tell her I was on my way to see where the fuck Ryan was at.

Before I left the house, I made sure that Malcolm and Ashanti were tucked in tight. I kissed them both on the cheeks before I dipped out. I pulled out my phone and turned on the GPS to locate Ryan's phone. I punched in the address on my GPS screen. The address and direction appeared on my car's GPS system within seconds. It didn't take me no time to realize the location. Arriving at Ryan's law firm, his second home, I saw his car and several other vehicles beside his BMW. There were no more spots to park at the firm, so I decided to park at the store that was located in the same parking lot by Ryan's firm. I took a deep breath because I had no clue what was about to go down. I popped my trunk so I could grab Malcolm's aluminum bat. I told myself whatever bitch he was creeping with was about to feel my rage. As I walked to the entrance, my head was spinning and my palms were sweating.

My heart was beating as if I had run a marathon, and the hairs on my neck were tingling. I made it to the front entrance, but it was way too dark inside. It was one light on, and it was impossible to see what going on. I knew someone was in the back because I could see a shadow. I pulled on the door handle, but it was locked.

I banged on the window as hard I could. My intention was to bust through the door with the bat, but logic kicked in. I pulled out my phone to try calling Ryan, but I got no luck there. It went straight to the voicemail. Now I was hot and frustrated. I knocked on the door one more time before I kicked that bitch. I ran my hand down my face and proceeded back to the car. On my way to the car, I noticed a figure coming in my direction. I knew it had to be a man because of the size. I gripped the bat tight because if he tried some crazy shit, I was ready to Barry Bond his ass. The figure had on a black hoodie so I couldn't see their face. I kept my head down as I continued walking towards my car. The figure paused for a second and my heart began to tremble like crazy. He reached for the top of his hood to reveal his face. My heart dropped to the ground.

CHAMP

THIRTY MINUTES EARLIER

Ring, Ring!

"Yo," I groaned into the phone.

I glanced at the clock on my nightstand to see exactly what time it was.

"Champ!" I looked at the screen and was shocked to see Trina's name.

"Get up, Champ!" Trina yelled in the phone.

"What's going on!?"

"Faith's running a high temp, and she needs some medicine." I heard Faith coughing in the background.

I was so tired, but I had to do what I had to do for my baby girl. I glimpsed at the clock one more time then told Trina give me about an hour so I could run to the store. I hung up the phone then exhaled. I threw on my wife beater, black sweatpants, and white Nike shoes. When I stepped out the door, the night breeze hit me. I grabbed my Oakland Raider hoodie quickly and put that bitch on. I hated any type of cold chill. Before I got in my car, I popped the hood because I knew I would need some water. I was just about to hop in my car when my phone began to ring.

When I glanced down at the screen, it was Roshika calling. I just ignored it. I really wasn't feeling shawty like that anymore. Lately, she had been calling and texting a nigga all day and night. As I drove through town, I was relieved that there were hardly any cars on the road, so it didn't take me long to pull up at the nearby convenience store, which was located right beside a law firm. There was no way I was about to drive all the way to Walmart for no medicine. I parked next to an ocean blue Monte Carlo with dark tint. There was music blasting and I could have sworn I smelled some weed in the air.

I threw the car into park, grabbed my wallet out the glove compartment, walked up to the convenience store, and prayed that they had some medicine for Faith. If Faith wasn't ill, I definitely wouldn't be out this damn late. I would be home in my bed like everyone else. I always made sure to scan my surroundings, so as I walked through the parking lot, I noticed there were hardly any cars around and the store looked bare as hell, but at least their sign still read open. As I was walking up to the store, I noticed a woman coming my way holding something in her hand. First thing that came to my mind was somebody done got fucked up or was about to get fucked up. As I got closer, I recognized the woman. I took off my hood, revealing my face.

"Sasha!" I said in a shocked tone.

When she recognized me, I saw the embarrassment in her eyes.

"What are you doing out this damn late, and why the hell you got a bat?" I asked, looking down at the bat with a raised eyebrow.

"Long story," she confessed as she brushed her hair to the side.

"Well, whatever going on with you, don't do nothing crazy," I warned her.

When I got locked up, I really learned a lot of shit. It taught me a lot about people messing up their life by reacting off their emotions.

She leaned up against some car and dropped the bat on the ground. I could see the pain in her eyes. She was battling something real serious. For a person to be raising hell in the middle of the night, especially a woman if they were doing some off the wall shit, then most of the time it was over a man.

I picked the bat up off the ground and handed it back to her.

"Thank you," she said, reaching for the bat.

"Don't let a man have you out here like this," I stated as I released my grip from the bat.

"Who said it was over a man?" she replied sarcastically. I just gave her a stare like 'really.'

"I can't judge you," I said, lifting up her face. Staring into her eyes, I saw the sorrow that she was battling inside.

"This ain't me," she confessed, and she swung the bat back and forth against the surface of the ground.

"I understand. Sometimes love has us doing all types of crazy things," I admitted.

I told her about the time I drove all around town looking for Trina one night. Come to find out, she was at school the whole time. We stood there talking about different things about life. She was a real down to Earth woman with a decent mind frame. When I glanced at my clock, we had done talked for over an hour. I told her I had to leave because I had only come to the store to grab my daughter some medicine. Sasha told me that she thought that was sweet that I got up in the middle of the night to go to the store for medicine.

"Thank you for listening to me, and thanks for talking some sense into me."

"No problem. If you ever need to talk, I'm here to listen. Don't forget we meet at the Turtle Park."

"I will be there," she assured me. I waited for her to hop in her car before I headed into the store. After I bought the medicine, I headed to Trina's house, but all I could think about was Sasha and the conversation that we had just had. I prayed that shawty got her mind right because it would be a shame that someone that pretty had to go through some crazy shit with a no-good nigga. Just seeing the pain in her eyes showed me the effect a man has over a woman. Pulling up to Trina's crib felt different as hell. I hadn't really been over here in a while. Since Jerome found me an apartment, I had no need to come over here. I picked Faith up from school and Trina came over and scooped her up from my place, Monday through Fridays. I slowly walked up the steel staircase. As I approached the door, I slightly knocked on the door and within seconds, Trina was standing there with a stank look on her face.

"I'm glad this wasn't a life or death situation," she scowled.

"I got caught up," I confessed as I pulled the medicine out my pocket.

She snatched it and closed the door right in my face. I was about to knock back on the door and give her a piece of my mind, but I was too damn tried to be fussing with Trina at the moment. I just proceeded back to my car, but right when I was about to open the door, I saw a shadow coming in my direction. My heart skipped a beat because I knew how the stick-up game worked.

"Damn, nigga ... It's like that now?" a female voice asked.

When I turned around, Roshika was standing with her black long trench coat which was opened wide, showing me her birthday suit. I raised an eyebrow at her because I already knew this bitch was acting crazy about the dick. I didn't even want to ask her how in the hell she knew where I was at. Instead, I threw up my hand and left her ass standing there like she was crazy.

SASHA

What He Don't Know Won't Hurt

"Girl ... tell me more about him," Sweet Pea said as she flipped through the channels.

"He's just my personal trainer," I mumbled as I tried to avoid going into too much detail. She powered down the television and turned in my direction.

"Spill the tea, bitch," Sweet Pea urged me.

I tried to hide shit from Sweet Pea, but she had that power of making me confess everything.

"Damn, I will tell you," I commented as I smiled at her crazy ass.

"Girl ... well, all I got to say is he very nice and sweet."

Sweet Pea was practically drooling from the mouth as she waited for me to go deeper in my description.

"He is a perfect gentleman," I added, snatching the remote out her hand.

"Bitch! Fuck all that ... Is he fine?" she asked.

"He alright..." I slowly said.

To be real, he was fine as hell. I wasn't about tell her that part though. Sweet Pea was my girl, but certain shit you just don't reveal.

"When can I meet him?" she asked curiously.

Nikalos   128   Solakin Publications

I became silent because there was no way I was about to let Sweet Pea meet him at all.

"Never..." I playfully said as I began to flip through the channels.

I made a silly face at Sweet Pea and we both burst out laughing.

"On the real though..." Her face got earnest instantly. "...You really think Ryan stepping out on you?" she asked.

"What make you think I believe Ryan is stepping out on me?" I asked her with a confused expression on my face.

Sweet Pea shook her head at me before she gave me a stern look.

"You asking me that question really hurt my damn feelings. Bitch, don't even fucking play with me. I've noticed how you been acting all strange and shit, and that little stunt you did the other night really had me thinking something was up with you. You can't hide shit from me, Sasha. I've been your friend since day one, so I know you better than anyone."

Right at that moment, I really didn't know how to respond. I just had a dull expression on my face. Instead of entertaining Sweet Pea, I turned my attention back to the TV.

"If you want to talk about it, you know I will listen," Sweet Pea insisted.

"Thanks, Sweet Pea, but Ryan and I are just fine."

But I knew deep down inside that I was once again lying to myself. But I'd rather lie than to face the reality that my worst fear was indeed true.

I was relieved when I finally found a movie on TV because I wasn't in the mood to talk about my marriage at the moment. As we watched the movie Waiting to Exhale, I just thought about so many different things. My mind was playing wild, crazy tricks on me. I had so many "what if" statements circling in my head. What if Ryan was really cheating on me? What if he had another family on the side?

The more I watched the movie, the more I saw Ryan's face lying with another female. All of a sudden, my mind started to do something I wasn't expecting it to do. Thoughts of Champ came playing around in my head. For the last couples of nights, I had been thinking about him a lot. He had been there for me whenever I needed somebody to talk to, which had given me some kind of a relief to get some type of male point of view about my situation.

The sound of my cell blasting Migos pulled me from my wild thoughts.

"Hello," I said into the phone.

"Aye, baby." I looked at the phone and I didn't recognize the number or voice because all I could hear was a lot of static on the line.

"Who this!" I yelled into the phone.

"This Ryan."

"Ryan, why are you calling from a different number?" I asked curiously.

"My cell went dead. I forgot to charge it up last night. I left some important documents on the nightstand this morning. I need for you to bring it down to the courthouse as soon as possible," he instructed.

I rolled my eyes because I swear this nigga would lose his head if he didn't have it attached to his body. He was forever leaving shit, or losing something.

"Alright. I will be down there in a few minutes. Let me put some clothes on," I said, tossing the remote in Sweet Pea's lap.

"Where you running off to?" Sweet Pea asked.

"That was Ryan. He wants me to drop some documents off at the courthouse."

"Okay, cool. Well, can I catch a ride with you? I need to head over to Rodney's sister house for a quick second."

"Okay, you know I got you."

I headed towards the bedroom and went where he said the documents were located. I picked them up and placed them in my bag. All I wanted to do was stay home and chill. I wasn't planning on doing anything today. My body was aching from that intense workout Champ had me on.

I walked to my closet so I could grab me something comfortable to wear. Once I dropped the documents off, I had to drop Sweet Pea off at Rodney's petty ass sister's house. I didn't like his sister because she was the type of broad that kept up bullshit. She constantly planted crazy ideas in Rodney's head and told him lies, like the kids Sweet Pea had weren't his. I told Sweet Pea plenty of times I would've been beat that bitch's ass. I swear Sweet Pea was stuck on stupid when anything involved Rodney. I wished that any of Ryan's family members tried some shit like that about Malcolm and Ashanti; I promise they would see the old Sasha, and I wouldn't show any of them hoes any mercy.

When I emerged from the shower, I was feeling a lot better. I had found a cute little outfit to wear: a bright green John Deere T-shirt with a yellow tractor, denim shorts, a white pair of Pumas, and you know my favorite shades. Before I threw the glasses on, I made sure my makeup was on point. I wasn't a huge fan of the makeup trend. I loved my cute skin, but every now and then, I would dab on a little makeup just for the hell of it. I applied some lip-gloss, then I applied a little eyeshadow to finish the touch, and I was ready to head out.

I heard Sweet Pea snoring on my way down the stairs.

"Sweet Pea!'" I yelled, shaking her so she could wake up.

She jumped up and wiped the drool from her mouth. I just shook my head.

"Girl, come on!" I said as I helped her tote her things to the car.

I could tell it had to be a trial week because there were so many cars and hardly anywhere to damn park. I made sure to text Ryan to let him know I was outside.

I finally found a parking spot by the tax place, which was located beside the courthouse. Sweet Pea was knocked out yet again, so I bumped her to let her know I'd be right back.

She just threw up her hand to let me know she heard me. I hopped out and made my way across the street in no time. Downtown Albany, you had to be careful because these policer officers would try to give you a ticket for anything, especially jaywalking. I moved through the crowd swiftly, making my way to the courthouse. Once I made it to the top of the stairs, Ryan emerged from the courtroom door with a smile on his face. Ryan was looking good in his Armani fitted navy-blue suit with some black Fendi dress shoes. He stayed looking like money and always had some bitch smiling in his face.

"Hey baby. Thank you for bringing the documents to me," he murmured as he examined the documents.

"No problem," I assured him as I fixed his tie straight.

He gave me another kiss on the lips before he told me he had to get back to work. I wished him good luck on the case, but right when I was about to walk away, the courthouse door came open. Me and that little black bitch made eye contact. I lost it.

"What the fuck she doing here?" I asked Ryan with attitude.

"Let me explain, Sasha." He held his hand up, trying to calm me down. Instead of making a scene, I just dipped out before I beat that hoe's ass. I was furious. All this time I thought he was going to come to his senses and fire this bitch, but she was still working with him like nothing had happened. I wanted to just punch the smirk off that thot's face. My mind was going a mile a minute. I was so damn pissed off that I could barely see straight. I needed someone to talk to at this very moment because if I didn't, I was going to end up catching a charge. I pulled out my cell and called the one person I felt I could talk to.

"Yo," Champ groaned into the phone.

"Do you feel like talking?" I asked as I crossed the street.

"You know I'm here if you need me."

Just hearing him say that statement really did something to me.

After he had given me the place we could meet up at, I headed back to my car to find Sweet Pea was wide awake. I dropped her off at Rodney's sister house and headed to meet Champ.

CHAMP

A FEW WEEKS LATER….

For the last the few weeks, I had been in a crazy web dealing with all these women in my life. If I was not running mad dick in Yolanda, I was running from Roshika's Looney Tune ass. I did have to admit that shawty had a couple bolts missing from her cranium. I was also trying to help Sasha solve her problem with her husband. On top of all that, the one that get under my skin the most was bipolar Trina. One minute, she would let me stop by, then some days it would be like World War III with her. It seemed like every time we were around each other, we tended to have argument after argument, and none of them had a significant value. Faith was the only female that kept me balanced. That little girl be having me rolling all the time and helped me get through the day.

Knock, Knock!

I groaned as I got off my couch and headed towards my front door.

When I swung the door open, I saw Sasha. She was standing there with a blank expression on her pretty face. I opened the door wide to let her come inside. She walked in, sat on my couch, and placed her hands in her face. My apartment was not that big or small. It was a two-bedroom, one bath, and the kitchen and living room were connected together. I had the basic things a single man would have in his apartment. My living room area was designed very simple with two leather couches that aligned up along the right side of the room. Facing the two leather couches was a 50-inch flat screen TV that was mounted to the wall. A long wooden coffee table with two baskets underneath sat in the middle of the floor, that contained several Muscle & Fitness magazines and a bowl of candy on top. When you stepped into the kitchen, there was small picture of me and Faith posted up on the counter. My counter was loaded with different basic household appliances like a toaster, blender for my fruit drink, a microwave, and a basket filled with different fruits that Faith loved to eat when she came over. I looked over at Sasha and my heart broke for her. I hated when a woman was hurting.

"What's on your mind?" I asked as I took a seat and turned off the television so I could give her my undivided attention.

"Champ ... I have so much on my mind." I gave her the gesture that I was listening.

"It's getting worse every day. He ain't the same Ryan I met ten years ago. He used to put me first, now we barely even speak. I remember when I used to be able to look into his eyes and know that I was the only woman in his life. Now it's like I'm competing with everyone one else just for his attention," she explained as she wiped the tears from her eyes.

Seeing a woman crying did something to me every time. I started thinking about the times I used to cheat on Trina, and now I understood how she truly felt and all the tears that she had cried.

"Damn, shawty ... that's fucked up," I commented.

"I've been so loyal to him that it doesn't make sense."

"I got one question to ask you." She sobered up from her crying and gave me her undivided attention.

"Since that day I ran into you at the movies and over these past few weeks, I have gotten to know you, but I still can't get this thought out of my mind. I'm just curious to know why did that dude want to hurt you that day?" I asked.

I saw shame and embarrassment as she stared back at me.

Sasha didn't speak at first; instead, silence followed my question.

"It's a lot you don't know about me." She paused, looking at the ceiling. "My past will change your views of me," she confessed.

Right when she was about to continue, I stopped her in her tracks.

"Sasha, I'm not here to judge you. I have done a lot of shit in my life that I'm not proud of. Everybody has a deep past, some more terrible than others, but everybody goes through something," I preached.

"I understand, but my—" I cut her off again.

"If this is too much, you don't have to tell me," I stated honestly.

I could tell this was a tough issue she had dealt with.

"It's something about you that makes me feel comfortable. I feel I can trust you."

Damn, she had a nigga feeling all special and shit.

She took a deep breath then asked me was I ready. I just nodded my head. She then broke down her whole life story. Throughout the story, she had to stop because her emotions got the best of her. When she told me about her uncle molesting her when she very young, I thought that was the sickest thing a person could do. I mean, why the fuck would anyone want to mess with kids? How can a person prey on innocent children? Just looking at how smart and sexy she was, I never would have guessed that she was forced to live on the streets and sell her body. I found out that Geno was the nigga that had gotten her hooked on drugs and had her sprung out until she got control of her life.

I held her close to me as she cried on my shoulder. After she was all cried out, Sasha pulled away and wiped her tears from her eyes.

"Thanks for listening to my problems," she uttered as she stood up from the couch.

"I bet you thinking I'm one crazy bitch," she joked.

"Shid ... you good, ma," I assured her as I walked her to the door.

"I have to go pick up the kids from school, but I feel so much better. I really needed to get a lot of shit off my chest."

"Anytime you need me, I will be here," I whispered in her ear before placing a soft kiss on her cheek.

Our eyes connected for only a moment before she caressed my cheek and placed a kiss on my left cheek in return.

Some men wouldn't give a shit about Sasha or the insecurities that she was feeling inside, but I was a different type of nigga now, and I wanted Sasha to understand that I was going to be here for her when she needed me.

I watched as she waved goodbye and hopped into her car. Her scent had a nigga mesmerized, and I couldn't help but caress my cheek where she had leaned in and gave me a kiss. After her car had disappeared out of my driveway, I grabbed my keys because it was time for me to head to Faith's school so I could pick her up.

SASHA

I was leaving Sherwood Middle School from picking up Ashanti and Malcolm school. The whole time I was sitting in the parking lot, Champ was heavily on my mind. All I could think about was how wonderful of a person he was. He was different from most men. I really didn't give a lot of niggas my attention outside my marriage because they'd only want one thing and that was sex, but with Champ, it was different. His whole mind frame was so incredible. He was caring, honest, nurturing, and a great listener. He never looked at me sideways when I expressed things with him. He was the only person I ever felt comfortable opening up about my past with.

I loved the fact we could talk about anything, from sports to the grain of dirt on the ground. He was so intelligent that it blew the top off my cranium. He knew how to break life down to the smallest element. When he told me he had been incarcerated for nine years, that shit fucked me up.

Even though he had been locked away a good part of his daughter's life, he still managed to get out and be a great father. Most of the time, he talked about his daughter and how much he loved her whenever he and I were around one another. I found that so unique. Most men around his age were some deadbeat ass niggas. Champ was my stress reliever from life and the many insecurities that I was dealing with.

"Ma, can we go to Pizza Hut?" Ashanti asked with so much excitement in her voice. Ashanti handed me a few Pizza Hut coupons and told me that the school gave them to everyone that made all A's on their report card. Ashanti was no big fan of school, but she did make good grades. She knew Ryan gave them anything they wanted, especially when they excelled in school.

"I guess we can eat pizza today."

I made a right on Stuart Avenue and put the coupons in my lap. It had been a while since I'd done something with them. I'd been so caught up in Ryan's ass that I had been neglecting my kids.

"Malcolm!" I called out.

He put down his tablet and turned my way.

"Is everything going okay with you?"

Lately, Malcolm had been being distant from everybody.

"Yes, everything's good, I guess," he replied pitifully as he gave placed his attention back to his tablet. Malcolm had been in a slump since he had to quit basketball. I really prayed his condition got better because I hated seeing him like this. I wish there was something I could do.

"Things are going to get better," I assured him.

Kmart was the first spot we stopped at. I had to grab a few things for the house. Plus, I had to make sure I had some supplies for Malcolm's and my birthday. Our birthday was about three weeks away. I was going to throw a small cookout in the backyard. It wasn't going to be nothing too big or fancy. Ashanti felt like this was going to be a good opportunity to beg me to buy her some dolls. She knew I wasn't going to say no. Malcolm really didn't want anything, but I grabbed him a video game for his Xbox.

I was really surprised at the fact that it didn't take long in Kmart to get what I needed and get checked out. Usually, it took forever because it would be crowded as hell. We were in and out in no time.

It wasn't long before we finally arrived at Pizza Hut. The parking lot was swamped with cars, and I drove around twice before I found a parking space next to this white Honda Accord with 18-inch chrome rims. As soon as I opened the driver's side door, the smell of pepperoni and cigarette smoke invaded my nostrils. It was crunk as hell. Somebody was blasting Young Thug not far from where I was parked. I didn't recognize the song, but Ashanti knew some of the lyrics. I cut my eyes at her when Young Thug started cursing. She already knew not to say no curse words around me. She was only seven years old and was way too young to know

What He Don't Know Won't Hurt

anything about that type of music. I swear kids was growing up fast these days.

Pizza Hut was set up with a buffet in the middle of the floor, booths along the wall in a "L" shape with a couple of chairs, and tables placed in different areas. I shook my head as I noticed the drink machine that had 'out of order' on the Pepsi side. Damn, I'm glad I wasn't a damn Pepsi fan, I thought to myself. I told the kids to go find a table while I headed to the bathroom. I hated going in a restaurant's bathroom if it was dirty as hell. I swear that shit would ruin my appetite, and I would proudly leave and go somewhere else to eat. My bladder was on full due to all that water Champ had me drinking. When I finally made it back to the table, Malcolm was talking to some young girl. She looked familiar, but I couldn't put my finger on it.

"Malcolm, who that little girl was?" I asked when she walked away.

"His girlfriend!'" Ashanti yelled out.

"Shut up!" Malcolm said, trying to hit Ashanti. She just continued to laugh.

"Leave your brother alone, chile."

Looking at Malcolm interact with the little girl was kind of cute.

Nikalos   144   Solakin Publications

"Do y'all know what y'all want to eat?'" I asked, looking at the menu.

After about five minutes, they both finally came to an agreement on what they wanted to eat.

"Hello, I will be your waiter today. Are y'all ready to order now, or do you need more time?" the waiter asked as he took out his tablet.

Our waiter's name was Elijah. If I had to guess his age, I would give or take about eighteen at the most. He still had the cute little baby face. He was about five feet eight inches tall, brown skin complexion, skinny as a stick, with short dreadlocks that didn't even touch his neck, and two miniscule earrings.

"We're ready to order."

Elijah nodded his head as I pointed to what we were having and handed him the coupon that Ashanti had given me. We sat there talking and laughing as we waited on the food to come back. While we were sitting there, the little girl kept coming over, talking to Malcolm. He was trying to play like he didn't like her, but I saw it in his eyes that he was feeling her. At that age, females were way more mature than boys. When I heard the dark-chocolate woman call out for her daughter, I looked up and I knew it had to be her mother because they looked so much alike.

Ashanti was quiet and Malcolm was in his own little world, which gave me time to think about my life in silence. These last past few weeks had been very difficult for me. My heart was with Ryan, but I couldn't stop thinking about Champ. I didn't know what was going on. All I knew is that I feel I was "Trapped Between the Two," I thought to myself. I was kinda lost at this moment, and my emotions were all over the place.

"Here you go, ma'am," Elijah announced, snapping me out of my trance.

"Thank you. Can we have some extra napkins, cheese, and red pepper, please?" I requested.

He was so polite. He immediately nodded his head as he reached into his apron and grabbed a handful of what I asked for. I told him thank you again, paid for the pizza, then gave him a nice tip.

I really enjoyed my kids today. After we finished eating at Pizza Hut, we headed back to the crib. As I drove home, I couldn't help but stare at them through the mirror as they slept peacefully in the back seat. As I turned down my street, my phone started vibrating. I told myself I would check it once I got home. I had a couple more blocks until I pulled up in the driveway. The sun had settled for the afternoon, so the weather was kind of cool. Some of my neighbors were sitting on their lawns being nosy as usual. The neighborhood kids were skating up and down the street.

When I pulled up in my driveway, I was shocked to see Ryan's BMW were there. I was shocked that Ryan was even home this damn early. I parked right beside Ryan's car before I woke Malcolm and Ashanti to let them know we were home. I grabbed my purse and keys and headed into the house.

The kids screamed their daddy's name and he gave them both a hug and kiss before they both disappeared in their rooms for the night.

"Aye, baby," Ryan greeted me with a rose and teddy bear.

"I know I've been fucking up lately, haven't been giving you any of my time, and I just want to say I'm sorry for all that," he confessed, making my heart do cartwheels.

"Awww, baby."

I grabbed the teddy bear and rose then gave him a kiss as he led me to the couch.

"Sasha, you my world. I wouldn't trade you for the nothing," he confessed.

My feelings were all over the place.

"I love you more than life itself." He kissed me one last time; this time it was more passionate. I grabbed his face, brought it back to mine and didn't hesitate to slide my tongue down his throat.

"Meet me in the room in five minutes," I whispered as I blew him a kiss. Before I went in the bedroom, I peeped into Malcolm and Ashanti's room. Ashanti was playing with her dolls and Malcolm was sleep. I proceeded to my bedroom and strip to my bra and panties. I was so horny it didn't make no sense. It had been about two weeks since I allowed Ryan to touch me. When he tried to touch me, I made up some crazy excuse like I had a yeast infection or I wasn't feeling well. I knew that it sounded harsh, but it was what it was.

When I heard the door squeak, I knew Ryan was standing behind me. I just gestured for him to come get him some. Ryan pushed me on the bed, climbed on top of me, and allowed his tongue to roam my body. He started at my head, and within seconds, he was sucking the inside of my pussy. The way his tongue was rotating inside me had me begging for more.

"Shitt!" I yelled, grabbing the collar of his shirt. That shit felt so good, I didn't want it to stop.

I opened my legs as wide as I could. He used that to his advantage.

"Fuck me, daddy," I begged him.

I whimpered when he inserted his dick inside me and began to move back and forth real steady. I pulled him close to me as I began to whisper sweet things in his ear. My inside was on fire for him. He leaned down and slid his tongue into my mouth. Our tongues danced with one another. I felt his nature swelling inside of me. I put my arms around him he as he concentrated on pleasing my sweet spot.

"Yessss ... mmm…" I moaned out, digging my nails in his back.

"You like that, baby?" he asked, breathing heavily.

"Yes, daddy. I luv it," I cried out as I encouraged him to speed up.

I grabbed the lower part of his back, letting him know to give me more.

Ryan flipped me over as he kissed me all up and down my sweaty back. His lips slowly pressed up and down my back which sent chills down my spinal cord. I tooted my ass up, as he opened my ass cheeks then went back to work. He loved sexing me from the back; that was one his favorite positions. He was stroking back and forth with so much aggression that my clitoris was trembling, I reached down and caressed it back and forth as he continued to slam his dick into me.

"Shitttt! Baby ... dis dick sooo good ... shhhh!" I screamed out, closing my eyes as he pulled my hair. I was enjoying every minute of his loving. I bit down on my lip, wishing that he didn't have to stop.

"Who does this pussy belong to?" he asked aggressively, smacking me on my ass.

"Mmm .... you, daddy!" I screamed out as I bit down on the pillow.

He was going crazy on me, and I was loving that shit.

"Cha-" I immediately cut myself off, falling to the bed. I was tripping real hard. I was praying in the back of my head he didn't hear me. Within minutes, he was nutting all over my back. I just laid there with a perplexed expression.

CHAMP

The sky was bright and beautiful, and the wind was blowing lightly across the trees. I was sitting on my porch daydreaming about how things had happened in my life. I was very proud of myself. A year ago, I was sitting in prison, but now I had my own apartment and a great job that I loved. Life couldn't get better. Today I was supposed to be hanging out with Dre. He told me that he wanted me to hold something for him. First thing that came to mind was drugs, but he assured me it definitely was nothing illegal. I told him numerous times that life wasn't for me anymore. I was out of prison and I wasn't trying to do anything else to go back there.

Whenever I saw Dre today, that was going to give me the opportunity to talk to him about Sasha. I really didn't have anyone to vent to about shawty. I didn't see myself trying to date her because for one, she was married and I didn't deal with married women. My theory was if she did her husband like this, imagine what she would do to me. While I waited on Dre to pull up, I pulled out my phone and shot a text to Sasha. Lately, she and I had become texting buddies.

Me: Wasup!! (sent 9:45 a.m.)

Sasha: Nun, just get home folding some clothes up now. What you got going on dis morning? (received 9:47 a.m.)

Me: Shid...I got a basket full of clothes want 2 fold mines lol! On the real I'm just sittin on the porch drinking a beer waiting on my boy to come over (sent 9:52 a.m.)

Sasha: Uh... no I really don't want to fold these up. Drinking a beer early this morning huh? what you doing later? (received 9:55 a.m.)

Knock, Knock!

I placed the phone in my pocket so I could answer the door. When I swung it open, Dre was standing on my porch and had a PlayStation under his armpit. He was sweating bullets down his face. He pushed past me and went straight to the kitchen. He threw back of big cup of ice and wiped his mouth with the back of his hand.

"Bruh, you alright?" I asked, closing the door.

Since I'd been in my own place, Dre stopped by whenever he was in the neighborhood.

"Yeah, just been ripping and running all morning," he said as he brushed off his clothes.

Dre was rocking a black t-shirt, 8732 denim jean, Timberlands, and black fitted cap with E.M.F. across the front. He was clean, I had to give that to him.

"You still working out with that shawty?" he asked as he opened up his corn chips while flopping down on my couch.

"Yeah, I am."

"I'm surprise you ain't hit dat yet."

"One thing the streets taught me was to never mix business with pleasure," I said, snatching the bag out his hand.

"I hear you," he muttered as he began flipping through the channels.

"You know Trina gone kick yo' ass." He burst out in a hysterical laugh.

"Trina be on some other type of shit," I explained.

I explained how Trina had been playing a nigga to the left. I knew she was going to come around sooner or later; until then, I was just going to continue doing me. We watched a couple of segments on ESPN about LeBron and Dwayne teaming back up. Dre was a true Atlanta Hawks fan to death. I teased him all the time about how they weren't going to ever win a championship. I was huge LeBron James fan to the heart. Whatever team he was on, I was down with him. As we joked and talked, I told him more about old girl and how she be having me open. Dre was joking and telling me that she had a nigga fucked up. I couldn't lie; I was thinking about her on a constant basis.

"Bruh, I would stay longer, but I got to go because you know how the streets be. My presence is needed at all times. I really don't feel like peeling a nigga's cap back today," he said, giving me some dap.

"Go handle your business, Bruh."

I gave him a brotherly hug and dapped him up.

"Be careful out there, and what you want me to do with the PlayStation?" I asked as I examined the box.

"That's for my little nephew. His birthday coming up, just hold it for me."

I nodded my head as I watched him jump into his whip and pull off. Today he was pushing a black-on-black Buick Regal. Damn, I swear this nigga had a new car every time I saw him. I pulled my phone back out and noticed I had a bunch of messages that I hadn't had the chance to read.

Sasha: Poor baby done drunk his self to sleep. Hit me up when you get a chance (received 10:15 a.m.)

Yolanda: call me when you have time (received 10:16 a.m.)

Roshika: You a low down piece of shit. I hope yo lying ass go back to prison dumb ass nigga (Received 10:25 a.m.).

Roshika: I'm so sorry…. I just want some dick. (received 10:26 a.m.)

I just smirked at Roshika's message 'cause she was mad that I stopped dropping mad pipe to her. I would've kept fucking her, but shawty got too possessive of a nigga and wanted me to jump to her beat. She had started calling and texting me all throughout the night. I had told myself that I was going to change my number, but ain't really had time. Right when I was about to head to the bedroom, I heard a knock on the door.

When I opened the door, there stood Sasha. She was standing there looking so damn sexy. She had her hair slicked down with a pair of small gold hoop earrings. She was wearing a purple and white sundress, with some brown sandals, and looked like some Versace gold trimmed sunglasses. I just smiled because I was kind of happy to see her. She had a smile on her face as well.

SASHA

His blazing cold air conditioner hit me right in my mouth once I stepped into Champ's apartment. He had Future's "No Matter What" pumping out of the speaker. I sat down on the couch that was closer to the television. I saw Champ had beer bottles everywhere around his apartment. He had a brand-new PlayStation sitting on the coffee stand. I didn't ask him anything about that because I knew guys loved playing video games. When Ryan and I first got together, all he did was sit in front of the TV and play the PlayStation or Xbox. I tried on many occasions to learn how to play, but it was never my thing.

"So, this is how you are living now?" I playfully asked, pointing at the mess on the floor.

"Ha! Ha!" He clapped his hand, letting me know I had threw some slick shots at him. We had this thing where we always were making slick jokes towards each other.

"Nall, my partner came over. We had a few drinks. Matter of fact, he just left not too long before you knocked on the door."

I watched as he collected all the beer bottles off the floor and threw them in the trash.

"So, how is baby mama acting?" I asked as I stood up and started to help him clean his place up a little.

"Did y'all come up with a solution to y'all little issue?"

"Hell nall! Trina still on that bullshit."

I could tell that it affected him a lot because of how his demeanor changed when I said her name. One thing I knew about Champ was that he wanted a family, but everything had a time limit. He was going to have to learn that the best thing to do was not pressure Trina and just go with the flow of things.

"She's going to come around 'cause you a good man, Champ. Just give her time."

Champ nodded his head at my statement and pulled me into a hug.

"Thanks. I guess I needed to hear that."

If I wasn't married, I swear he would be someone I would want to spend the rest of my life with. He had everything that a woman needed in life. When we pulled away from our hug, I stood back, leaned up against the wall, and watched his every move. He was looking so damn sexy that it was making me feel some type of way. He was wearing a wife beater that was hugging his body just right. I knew he was packing because when we worked out, I saw his dick print plenty of times through his gym shorts.

When he brushed past me, I couldn't take it anymore. His body was calling me, and I answered on the first the ring. I aggressively grabbed him by the face and slid my tongue down his throat. He didn't deny me, so I relaxed as our tongues began to make love to each other. Kissing him was like a breath of fresh air. He pushed me against the wall which turned me on to a point where I was ready to give him my life. His hands roamed up my dress, touching my bare skin. His hands were so soft and gentle and gave me goosebumps. I closed my eyes as his hands and mouth roamed over my entire body. I placed soft kisses all over his neck as I caressed his cheek.

A few moments later, he picked me up and placed me on the counter. Glasses crashed to the floor, but we paid them no mind. I wrapped my arms around him, driving my tongue back in his mouth. He lifted my dress up while spreading my legs wide. He pulled my black thong to the side as he began to caress my clitoris. That shit sent all types of electricity throughout my body.

"Mmm..." A soft moaned escaped my mouth. I was soaking wet; you could see the moist wet spots through my panties. He ripped my thong off my body and threw them on the floor. I was feening for him to punish this pussy. I reached down and grabbed a handful of his rock-hard dick. I was ready for him to put it inside me. I wanted all my deepest fantasies fulfilled. My body was screaming sex me to a point of no return. My body trembled as it anticipated for the pleasure it was about to receive. I ripped his wife beater open down the middle, and I was amazed at how sexy he looked. I ran one hand up and down his muscular abs as I used my other hand to get his pants down.

I moaned softly as I wrapped my arms around his neck. My whole body wanted to just love all over him. I screamed out when he slid all his dick inside me. Every time he stroked in and out of me, I wanted more and more. Right at that moment, he was my drug and I was already addicted to him. The sensational high I was on with him, was out of this world. I never wanted to come back to Earth. When he slid his dick out of me and lifted me off the counter, he laid me across the top of the wooden table, and that's when his head disappeared under my dress. My toes curled up when his tongue began prowling around my clitoris. If I was blindfolded, I would have sworn that his thick tongue was his dick.

"Mmm ... Champ!" I moaned out as I wrapped my hands around his head. The pleasure he applied to me was a mesmerizing feeling. His hands clutched my thighs aggressively which had a bitch wanting to faint. He took his thumb and caressed the top of my clitoris as I continued to moan out his name. I grinded my hips, knocking down what was left on the table to the floor. I could feel the pressure that was building up inside, and it wasn't going to be long before I creamed all over his face. He lifted his head up for air, and I took that opportunity to stare deep down into his soul. I leaned up, planting my feet on the floor. I turned around, bending all the way over so he could take this pussy.

"Mmmm ... Yess, Champ!" I screamed when he rammed that dick inside of me again. I rocked back and forth to let him know that I could handle him. I looked back at him while still throwing it back to him. I felt like I was on top of the world with him. The more he grinded inside of me, the more he was gripping my firm, soft ass. When he grabbed the back of my neck with a tight grip, I swear that shit turned me on so much that words couldn't describe the feeling. The only thing I knew was that I was satisfied.

I felt as if he already knew my body because he knew all the right places to touch, suck, and lick to make me cum.

"Damn this dick good." I could barely get the words out correctly as he continued to pound inside me.

"Is this dick good, baby?" he asked while thrusting deep inside me.

"Yessssss ... this dick is too good!" I yelled back. My pussy was soaking wet.

"Say my name!" he demanded.

"Champ ... Champ!" I screamed out.

I was so lit that I lost control of everything. I threw my ass back with so much force. It took him by surprise because he almost lost his balance.

"Sasha! Sasha! Sasha!" The more I heard my name, the more I moved my body.

Champ slammed into me one last time before he filled me with his cum. I laid down beside him and could barely move. I was exhausted and sweaty. I couldn't even remember the last time I had even had sex this damn good. All I wanted to do was lay in bed and sleep the rest of the day away but once my phone began to ring and I seen Ryan's name flash against the screen I knew that it was time for my ass to wake up and face reality. I was a married woman and I had just committed adultery. I slid out of bed just before I ignored

Ryan's phone call. I groaned when I noticed I had five missed calls.

"I have to go, my husband just called."

Champ slid out of bed and began to get dressed right along with me. After him and I was both dressed he placed a kiss on my lips as he walked me to my car. I was just about to hop in my car when Champ grabbed me by my arm.

"Sasha, are you good?"

"Yes, I'm fine. Why you ask?"

"Don't lie to me."

I tried to smile but my emotions was all over the place that I couldn't even fake it.

"I will call you when I get home," I promised champ before I hoped in my car and headed home.

As I drove towards my house I couldn't help but cry. Never had I ever cheated on my husband and I never wanted to until I met Champ. I felt horrible because I had just cheated on my husband and I had enjoyed the shit.

Soon as I pulled up at the house I noticed that Ryan's car was already there. I stepped out my car and headed inside the house to find Ryan siting in the living room watching T.V.

"Hey baby, what you doing home so early and where the kids at?"

"I've been calling you for an hour straight to tell you that I had made it home early and I was taking the kids to their friends house. I wanted us to get a day to ourselves."

"I'm sorry Ryan I didn't hear my phone ring."

I rubbed my hands through my mangled hair before I headed towards my bedroom. I wanted to hop in the shower as quickly as I could because I didn't want Ryan to smell another man scent on me. I closed the bathroom door behind as I stepped into the shower and begun to let the hot water beat up against my sexually satisfied body. I closed my eyes as images of Champ began to resurface in my brain. I slid my two fingers in and out of my kitty cat as I imagined Champs dick sliding in and out my pussy. I moaned out his name as I pleased myself. I didn't know what was up with me but all I could think about was fucking Champ. I felt like this nigga had cast a spell on me. After I had reached my climax I soaped my body up and down before rinsing myself clean.

When I stepped out the tub I noticed that my towel that I was going to use was no longer sitting on the bathroom sink and my bathroom door was wide open. I was just about to call out for Ryan to bring me another towel when he stepped into the bathroom. He was holding my towel and had a perplexed expression on his face. I could tell something was up which caused me to be on high alert.

"Can I have my towel?"

I shivered as the cool air hit my wet body.

After he had given me my towel I wrapped it around my body and was just about to step around him when he grabbed me by my arm.

"Sasha."

"What's wrong Ryan?"

I could tell how he was looking that he was angry about something.

"I just want to know one thing and whatever you do don't lie to me."

"Okay baby, you know I always have kept it real with you."

"Okay cool, I want you to explain to me why you was moaning another nigga's name while you was in the shower. I want to know who the fuck Champ is."

I froze and squeezed my eyes shut as I prayed for the best way to get myself out of this situation. As he eyes bored into my own I couldn't help but to look away.

SASHA

My mind was doing somersaults. I didn't know what to do. I knew I had to think of something fast, because his face was like the devil. I bit down on my bottom lip and dropped the towel, revealing my naked body.

I took that time and grabbed the bottom of his face and rubbed his chin with my thumb. His face was still balled up in anger. He snatched my hand away from him and looked me directly in the eye.

"So who the fuck is Champ?" Ryan asked aggressively.

I had never seen him this mad, ever, so I knew to choose my words very wisely.

"Baby, you are my Champ."

"What?" he asked.

He couldn't understand exactly what I meant, so I immediately ripped his shirt open to show him exactly what I was trying to tell him.

"Baby, I've been missing you so much. I couldn't control myself in the shower; please forgive me, baby. Champ is only a nickname that I call you when you aren't around."

I didn't give him time to respond before I slid my tongue into his mouth. When I felt his hands caress my body, I knew I had him exactly where I wanted him. When our faces detached from one another, I stared into his sexy eyes.

"Baby, come fuck me like a champ," I seductively whispered in his ear.

Ryan didn't hesitate to fulfill my request. He scooped me up in his arms, and we kissed until we made it to the bed.

One thing life has taught me was that sex was a man's weakness. My plan was real simple: I was going to put some good loving on him until he forget about the whole thing.

When we made it to the bed, my nerves were still bouncing everywhere because I still couldn't believe Ryan had heard me in the shower. When his hands started roaming my body, my pussy started dripping with anticipation. I immediately dropped to my knees and pulled out his manhood so I could please him with my mouth. I wrapped my hand around his massive rod then shoved it inside my mouth without any hesitation. As soon as it hit the back of my mouth, an untamed moan escaped my lips. My plan was working perfectly, which I was grateful for.

"You like that, baby?" I asked, removing his dick from my mouth.

Staring into his eyes, I could tell he was enjoying every moment of this hardcore blowjob. For the next couple of minutes, I allowed him to ram his dick in and out of my mouth. One thing I learned about Ryan was that he loved himself some good, wet pussy, but some bomb head had his ass weak as shit. I was going to suck every thought he had about me messing around out of his mind. I sat him on the end of the bed, spreading his legs, and began to suck him until all of his kids were going down my throat. I pushed him back on the bed, and he was just about to speak, but I stopped him in his tracks. Instead of him talking about irrelevant shit, I was ready to fuck.

I slid his nine-inch dick inside me and looked down at him as I moaned out his name.

"Shit!" I yelled out as I digged my nails into his chest.

I bounced up and down on his dick while he held my hips in place. In the back of my mind, as I stared into Ryan's eyes, I felt guilty as hell, but I quickly pushed the thoughts from my mind. I leaned down to suck his neck, but he caught me midway and slid his tongue into my mouth. Ours tongues connected just like old times, and images of our life began flashing before my eyes. Tears began to roll down my eyes. I knew that I had committed the ultimate sin. When he heard me sniffle, he stopped what he was doing then stared into my face.

"Baby, everything okay?" Ryan asked, wiping the tears from my eyes.

I didn't speak, just nodded my head because I didn't want to say some stupid shit. The more I tried to hold my emotions inside, the more tears started running down my face. Good thing Ryan had his eyes closed. I climbed off him and gave myself a pep talk before I started back giving him jaw dropping head. My juices were all over his dick, and I could taste myself as I sucked on the tip of his dick. After I had sucked him, I slid back on top of him and decided to do something different that I rarely ever did. I decided to surprise his ass with some anal sex.

I cursed gently as I slid him into my ass. The fact that I was on top of him helped with how much dick I wanted to go inside. Ryan caressed my titties as I played with my clit. The more I rubbed on my pussy, the more my ass muscles began to loosen up. I kept prancing up and down on his dick as his moans filled the room. His mouth began to tremble, so I knew he was soon about to reach his nut.

"Sasha!" Ryan moaned out, slapping my ass.

I increased my speed as he caressed my ass. My insides were on fire as him and I fucked one another.

"Baby, I'm about to cum!" he screamed.

I screamed when he shot his thick white cum into my ass.

He slid me off him before he slid his tongue into my mouth.

"I love you, baby," Ryan whispered in my ear.

"I love you too, babe," I mumbled before I laid down in his arms and fell into a deep sleep.

THE NEXT MORNING

As soon as I opened my eyes I felt the pain instantly. My back, side, thighs, pussy, and my ass were sorer then a muthafucka. I was so glad that I had talked my ass out of a tongue lashing by Ryan last night. That was the only serious thing that I was worried about. Seeing Ryan upset last night wasn't something that I was expecting.

I groaned as I finally got up the courage to move out of Ryan's arms towards my side of the bed. While he slept, I stared up at the ceiling. I knew deep down inside that I was dead ass wrong. I made up my mind that I was going to make things right. Whenever I saw Champ, I was going to tell him that we couldn't see each other anymore. Even though Ryan was cheating, two wrongs didn't make a right. I had too much to lose fucking with Champ.

I must have drifted back off to sleep because when I woke back up two hours later and rolled over, Ryan was nowhere to be found. I called out his name but got no response. My first thought was that he was downstairs, but the fact that I heard nothing coming from downstairs gave me every reason to take a look out my window. When I noticed that his BMW was gone, I quickly got an odd feeling that something wasn't right. Never did I ever wake up alone in bed; never did he leave the house without letting me know that he was going to be back. I tapped my finger against my check as I tried to refresh my memory to find out where the last place I had last seen my phone. I shot toward my bathroom and found it lying face down on the countertop. When I hit the power button, it didn't respond. I quickly ran back in the room searching for my charger. I plugged the phone and waited for a little while for the phone to get a enough juice to power back up. Once my phone had a little charge, I powered it back on, and that's when a bunch of text messages and notifications began to flood my phone. Most of the messages were from my home girl Sweet Pea telling me she needed to talk to me. I quickly responded back and told her okay, and I had to talk to her as well. I had a few messages from Champ. I read them and shot him a message telling him that I needed to talk to him about something important. Just when I was about to read my Facebook notifications, I heard a knock at my door.

Knock, Knock.

When I got to the bottom of the stairs, the knock became louder and harder. I knew it was early, but I didn't think to check the clock to see what time it was. When I swung the door open, I was shocked to see Tamara standing there.

"Good morning, girl," she greeted.

I noticed she had a concerned expression on her face.

"Good morning, Tamara. Everything okay with you?" I asked because rarely did Tamara ever come to my house.

"Yeah, I had called your phone, but it went straight to voicemail. I came over to check on ya to make sure you were good."

"My phone died, but everything is good."

Tamara cleared her throat.

"Well here is your plate back."

She handed me the plate, and I was definitely taken by surprise.

She must have noticed the shock on my face because she quickly added that Ryan had fixed her a plate last night.

"Girl, you sure got a nice husband."

I kept a smile on my face because I didn't want to reveal the fact that I was really frustrated at the moment. The fact that my husband had fed another bitch behind my back had me heated. Shit like this pissed me the fuck off. I hated a sneaky ass nigga.

"Yeah, girl, he too good," I said sarcastically.

"I wish Keon was like Ryan," she said as she walked to her charcoal Buick.

Tamara was Malcolm's friend mother and stayed right across the street in a three-bedroom house. Before she married Keon, she told me she had been in a horrible marriage with her last husband. She was a victim of abuse and wanted nothing more than to be happy again. Even though Keon didn't hit her, he did other shit that probably was fucking up their relationship. Half the time Keon was never home, and he was always cheating on her with some random bitch; at least those were the rumors that I heard around town.

They didn't have any kids together which was a damn blessing for her. The two kids that she had was from her last husband. Tamara worked part time at a small spa, and for the most part, she was a cool down to earth type of bitch, but I didn't trust that bitch around my damn man when I wasn't around. It wasn't because I was jealous and possessive of my Ryan; it was only because I always got a feeling that Tamara wanted Ryan for whatever reason. I knew I had a damn good husband, and other bitches knew that shit too.

I stepped back inside the house and tried thinking about what Tamara was slick trying to say about Ryan being such a good man. I was wondering why Ryan didn't mention anything about Tamara last night. I had learned early in life that if a nigga kept secrets about certain shit, then he knew deep down inside that he wasn't supposed to be doing the shit in the first place. Ryan knew how I felt about Tamara and him, and here he was going behind my back feeding this hoe. The fact that he wanted to eavesdrop on me last night but didn't tell me about what the fuck he was up to though, was what really irked my nerves. A nigga never eavesdropped unless he was feeling some type of guilt for something that he had done. The fact that he was talking to Tamara when I wasn't around had me feeling some type of way.

My mind began to race, and I began to get angry as fuck. I began to have all these crazy ass thoughts and hated the feeling. I was beginning to think that this nigga probably had this bitch in my fucking house last night without me even knowing the shit. He claimed he sent the kids away so we could have some alone time, but now I wasn't even buying that bullshit ass lie.

I quickly grabbed my phone and texted Champ to let him know that I was on my way to his crib. All I had to do was jump in the shower then I was going to head out. As I washed my body down with some Caress soap, I closed my eyes as I tried to do anything to take my mind off what Tamara had just told me. Just thinking about Champ always made me feel better. I moaned quietly as the soap hit my tender nipples. My body was aching for some good loving, and there was only one man who could fulfill my needs. I popped opened my eyes quickly when I realized that I had to hurry up and head over to his crib if I was still going to go.

Within twenty minutes, I was out the bathroom and smelling good as hell. I hurried to my closet and pulled out a pair of black leggings, a crème top, and a pair of my favorite black snow boots. I brushed my hair down before pulling it back in a ponytail and applying lip-gloss on my full lips. I stared at myself in the mirror to make sure I was looking decent before I grabbed my purse and headed out the door. I jumped in my car and proceeded to my destination without giving it a second thought.

CHAMP

2 WEEKS LATER

I had been complaining about how hot it was a few months ago, but now I was praying that the sun would hurry back up and come back out. It was colder than a muthafucka out the door. My fingertips felt like they were about to fall off. I was so glad that I had invested some money into getting me a new whip with some jet fuel heat and air. I was so tired of riding around in no heat or air in that bitch. I had finally gotten me a clean ass car. . Instead of spending all my money in fixing it up my Chevy, I decided to buy me a Tahoe from a nigga that I was working out with at the gym. He had recently gone to purchase him another car and sold me his all-black Tahoe.

The Tahoe was in great condition; I couldn't even lie about that shit. The only thing I hated about a Tahoe was that it fucked up some gas, but that was something that I was willing to look over. I only drove that bitch when I took Faith to school. The rest of the time, I drove my box Chevy which I dreaded but it did get me where I needed to go . There was no way I was going to just throw away my box Chevy, I mean I still drove it on the regular. I always made sure to show both my cars some love.

Today was Monday, and I had just picked my daughter, Faith, up from school. I loved picking my daughter up from school because Trina couldn't. I had been locked up so long and had dreamed about this moment for years. I promised myself just before I walked out of the prison doors that once I got out, I was going to be the best father that I could be, and here I was doing the very thing that I had dreamed of. My thoughts were interrupted when Faith called out my name from the back seat.

"Daddy!"

"Yes, baby," I said, turning down the music that I had blasting.

"I don't want to move, Daddy."

"Move?" I quickly said, making sure I was hearing her correctly.

"Yeah. Mom said we were going to move to Boston."

My heart was at a standstill for a second. I didn't know what to think or to say at the moment. I felt like Faith had hit me across the head with a brick. This wasn't something that I was expecting to hear today. I thought that today was going to be like any old day, but apparently, I had been wrong. This definitely had to be some kind of misunderstanding. I had no clue why Trina didn't mention nothing about she was moving to me.

I refused to let her take my baby girl from me, especially all the way to Boston. She got me all the way fucked up, I thought to myself. This couldn't be happening to me right now. I got to figure something out fast.

When I reached the red light, I turned my attention to Faith to let her know that I was going to fix the situation. I could tell that Faith felt a lot better after she heard me tell her that. The whole ride to Trina's cousin crib, I was saying everything that I could to make Faith understand that I wasn't about to let her leave me. As I comforted Faith, I also was comforting myself. The fear of losing my daughter when I had finally come back in her life, was what hurt me to my heart.

I had been so gone in my feelings that I was shocked when I pulled up at Trina's cousin house a few moments later. As I shut the engine off, I sat still for a few moments longer because I was still trying to get my mind right. Right now, my thoughts were still messing with me.

Why would Trina keep a secret like that from me? She knew I was still working on building a great relationship with Faith. I saw Faith at least four times a week. I was in her life, and I wanted it to stay that way.

"Faith."

She turned to me before unfastening her seat belt.

"Don't worry about nothing; Daddy with handle it, okay?" I ensured her again.

"Daddy, I know you will."

She leaned over and hugged my neck, and I kissed her on the forehead in return.

I loved my baby to death. She was the only reason why I hadn't snapped around this bitch.

"Don't give Alexis and them no problems."

"I won't."

"I love you."

"I love you more," she said.

Hearing my daughter say that put a smile on my face. I watched as Faith headed to the front door as I grabbed my phone to call Trina. Unfortunately, I had to hang up because an incoming call was coming through. It was Yolanda asking me if I would stop by before I headed back home. Even though my mind was in a million places, just hearing Yolanda's voice brightened my mood just a little bit.

I told Yolanda to give me a minute and I would swing by to see her. After I disconnected the call and hit Trina up again, I was disappointed when that didn't answer. I quickly left a voice message to let her know we needed to talk. When she got my voice message, I knew she would know that it was urgent and call a nigga back. I put my car in gear and took off toward Yolanda's crib.

When I pulled up at Yolanda's crib, I checked my phone to see if Trina had called me back. When I didn't see a phone call, I groaned with frustration. I hit the horn to let Yolanda know that I was outside. She didn't take long to emerge from the house with a bright smile on her face. I removed the keys from the ignition and threw my phone in the glove compartment. I jumped out and walked across

Yolanda's bright green grass. Yolanda and I had been kicking it kinda strong lately, but I wasn't crazy. I knew she and I would never be together, and it was strictly sex—nothing more than that. Yolanda was fine and all, but she wasn't girlfriend material. She could suck a dick so good it made a nigga's toes curl, but as far as making her my girl, that wasn't even in my plans.

As soon as I stepped on her small mini porch, she hugged me tightly before placing a kiss on my neck. She was smelling good as hell and her soft kisses calmed my nerves. Soon as she closed the door behind us, I slid my hand up her tank top and caressed her small b-cup breasts. Her nipples were pointing out at me as her lips made their way to my mouth, and I immediately threw my tongue inside her mouth. My hands caressed the rest of her body as I slid my finger to her sweet spot. She was moist between her legs which had me ready to dig deeper, but she quickly pulled my hands away.

"Hold up, Champ," she said softly.

"I need to tell you something," she mumbled as I began to kiss on her neck.

"Later, baby," I muttered against her neck.

She pulled away from me and pulled me down on the couch next to her.

I was a little irritated because right about now, all I wanted to do was get my dick wet. I wasn't in the mood to talk about no serious shit. I wanted to relieve some stress, not cause any more of it, but instead of rushing her to fuck, I decided to listen to what she had to say to me.

"What's up, Shawty?"

"Champ, you know I have been enjoying fucking with you these past few weeks."

I nodded my head in agreement because I had been enjoying us as well.

"I don't want you to be mad at me because I never would do anything to hurt you intentionally, but I just wanted you to know that me and my baby daddy decided to get back together."

I released my grip on her and quickly slid away from her.

"I'm sorry, Champ."

I cut her off.

"You good, Shawty," I said as I raised up from the couch.

She quickly grabbed my arm and begged me to not dip out.

"What I need to stay for?" I asked her with a fucked-up expression on my face.

I snatched away from her and headed toward the door.

She called my name out, but I didn't bother by turning around. I wasn't mad that she had gotten back with her baby daddy because every child needed both their parents, but I wasn't about to be the nigga that was trapped between the two of them. If I couldn't be first, I wasn't trying to be second.

As I walked to my car, I couldn't help but notice that I had been getting fucked up news all damn morning. I jumped in my whip, went straight to the liquor store, and that's when my whole life changed for the worst.

SASHA

I had been calling Champ phone all damn morning, but I never got an answer. That was not like him at all. I stopped by his house, but I noticed his Tahoe wasn't there, so I figured he must have been with his daughter. Later that day, I decided to head to the gym to see if he had made his way over that way, because it was getting late. As I rode down Dawson Road, all I could think about was Champ and how he made me feel.

I quickly turned on the radio so I could focus on something else. Every song that played slick reminded me of him. When Future blasted through the speakers singing "Incredible," my thighs started trembling to the beat. I turned the radio off and decided to let down the window so I could let the cold breeze hit my face.

Sasha, get yourself together, I told myself as I pulled into Jabo's gym.

Champ had started working at Jabo's gym two weeks ago. The last gym had closed down, so he was forced to get another job. I pulled out my phone and instantly got in my feelings when I noticed that Champ had not hit me back yet. Before I stepped out the car, I checked my appearance to make sure I didn't have nothing on my face or between my teeth. When I opened the door to the gym, the air and music were turned up to the max. I stepped to the front desk and that's when Tonya told me to hold on for a second.

Tonya and Champ both had dipped out and came to Jabo's gym when the old gym had closed down. Tonya was a down to earth chick. I had no problems with her. As long as she didn't do no crazy shit like try to seduce Champ, there was not going to be no beef with us. I could tell how she looked at Champ that she wanted his ass just as much as I wanted him, but as long as she just looked and not touch, I was cool with that.

My thoughts were interrupted when Tonya put down the phone and asked me what I needed.

"I don't need nothing; I was just looking for Champ. Is he here today?"

"No, he ain't here. I find it strange because he ain't even call in to tell me he wasn't going to show."

"Well, if he shows, can you let him know that I'm looking for him?"

"Okay, cool. I will let him know."

I was just about to walk off when Tonya told me that I was glowing.

"I ain't trying to get in your business and all, but are you expecting?"

I wanted to smack Tonya's nosy ass. I never noticed if I was glowing or not, but being pregnant was certainly out of the question. Champ and I had only messed around twice, but he always used a condom. I always stressed that he used one. There was no way I was ready to have another baby, especially when I was still married to Ryan.

I smirked at her and waved her off.

I wasn't in the mood to entertain Tonya because I already knew she wanted to get some type of details as to what type of relationship Champ and I truly had. All I cared about at the moment was where Champ was at, because I truly needed to talk to him.

I wrapped my body up in my cashmere sweater as I ran toward my car. When I heard my phone ringing, I instantly froze. My first thought was maybe this was Champ finally contacting me. I dug my phone out my purse and tried to hurry up and answer, but I was a little too late. When I checked my call log, I noticed whoever had just called me had a long crazy number. I groaned with frustration because there was no way that Champ was calling me from a number like that. I unlocked my car and hurried inside. Just when I was about to crank up my car, my phone started back ringing. It was that same crazy ass long number.

"Hello," I said with irritation

"You have a collect call from an inmate named 'Elijah Champion.' If you accept, push 1 and 9 to decline."

My heart stopped when I heard his name mentioned. I hit one as soon as the operator instructed me to. When I heard his voice, it melted me inside

"Baby, are you okay? What in the hell are you doing in jail? I asked him with concern in my voice.

"Baby, I just wanted to call to let you know I was okay. I got in a little trouble earlier today at the liquor store. I will tell you more about it later. Just come down and see me when you get the chance. You can come from two until four or seven until nine tonight."

"Okay, boo. I will be there at two to see you."

I looked over at the dashboard and noticed it was one thirty. After we hung up, I quickly punched the gear in drive and jetted down the street. All I was thinking was he must had done some crazy shit to be in the county jail. When I crossed the railroad tracks, I spotted the jailhouse on the corner. Every time I came near the county jail, I always got the creeps. I still remembered the time when I was younger that I almost found myself locked up behind bars, all because of a misunderstanding.

It was a Saturday night, and I was headed to go drop Malcolm and Ashanti off at their new babysitter's house. Ryan and I had major plans for the night. He had just won one of his toughest cases, and he wanted to celebrate. As I drove across the Lee County Line, I heard and just happened to notice sirens coming from behind me. In the back of my mind, I knew the sirens wasn't for me, at least that was what I was telling myself. Sadly, I was mistaken. A cruiser pulled up alongside me and instructed me to pull over to the shoulder. Malcolm and Ashanti kept asking what was going on, but I couldn't tell them anything because I didn't know myself. I pulled over, rolled down my window, and waited for the police officer to come to my car. I instructed Ashanti and Malcolm to play with their tablet, and I would handle everything else.

"Can you step out your vehicle, ma'am?" the white officer asked in a harsh tone.

"Excuse me, but what did I do, Officer?"

He didn't answer me; instead, he pulled open my door, pulled me out of my car, and pushed me face down on the ground. I didn't know what was going on. My heart was racing, and my body was trembling from fear. I had been watching all over the news about innocent people being killed by police officers. I began to silently pray that whatever was in this man's heart, he would let me be and leave me and my kids alone.

Tears fell from my eyes. When I tried to lift my head up, the white officer pushed my face into the moist grass.

"So you think we going to keep letting you bring drugs in this town?" the police officer asked.

"We finally got you now," the second officer whispered in my ear.

His breath was horrible, and it smelled like some old gym socks mixed with a pile of shit.

When I heard my babies crying out and yelling my name, I tried lifting up yet again, but the officer planted my head back into the grass. I couldn't do nothing at this point but cry. I laid there praying for my life. This was a dream and a horrible mistake. They must have had me confused with some other random bitch. They searched my car and found nothing but some diapers and baby formula.

A few moments later, I heard the officer's radio go off. Turns out they had finally caught the bitch who was trafficking drugs to Lee County. Apparently, the bitch had the same car as mine. When the officers finally realized that they had gotten the wrong woman, they finally let me up off the ground and tried to apologize for their huge fuck up, but I ignored their asses. Instead, I hopped back in my car and sped off. I wanted to get far away from them as possible. Lee County had nothing but corrupt cops, so when I took my ass up to the police department two days later to complain, nobody did shit.

And to this day, those police officers were still patrolling the streets. They didn't give a fuck about my husband being a highly paid lawyer. They were still racist to the fact a black man was so successful.

Ring, Ring.

The ringing of the phone brought me back to reality.

"Hello."

"Aye, baby, is you at home?" Ryan asked.

I almost slipped and said where I was at, but I was so glad that I thought better of that shit. Instead, I lied and told him that I was with Sweet Pea.

I definitely couldn't tell him I was in Lee County heading to the jailhouse to see the man that I was falling in love with.

"Okay, I wanted to spend a little time with you tonight."

"That will be fine, baby. I will love that. Let the kids stay the night with their friends tonight so we can get some quiet time," I told him sweetly.

Ryan quickly agreed before telling me he was heading back to work and would talk with me soon.

After we had hung up the phone, I pulled up at the jail house and headed inside. My heart was pounding the whole time as I got closer to the entrance. I took a deep breath and then opened the steel doors.

CHAMP

Shit! I can't believe this was happening to me again, I thought to myself as I stared at the white brick walls. All I could think about was the years I had spent in prison. I had told myself once I got out that I would never come back here. Everything was falling apart for me, and I had no idea how I was going to cope. I already was struggling with finding out that Trina was about to skip town with my baby girl, then Yolanda told me that she was planning on getting back with her baby daddy. I guess all them emotions that I was feeling had me in my feelings. The fact that I let a pussy ass nigga test me and land me in this hell hole only told me one thing: that I had lost control of my emotions.

Heading to the liquor store was a bad idea from the jump, but never did I think it would land my ass in jail. I groaned with irritation as I closed my eyes and began to think about what had gone down at the liquor store to land me in this jail cell.

I had just stepped into the liquor store to grab me a bottle of Henny, when I spotted Geno right in front of me. Our eyes locked on one another for a quick moment before he gave me that evil smirk. I wanted to knock the grin off his face but decided to just be the better person and dip the fuck out the store before one of us ended up dead. I could never forget a face, and Geno's face was unforgettable. I knew he had it out for Sasha from the moment I saved her ass from him when her and I first met. I was almost out the door when Geno came up from behind me and said some disrespectful shit.

"Can you deliver a message for me, nigga?" Geno asked.

He didn't even give me time to respond before he began to pop off at the mouth.

"Tell that little bitch you're fucking that I know where she lives, and I know her every move. Back in the day, I used to own that little bitch. I had her fucking, sucking, and doing all types of tricks before she broke free and got married. Make sure you tell her I want my fucking money that she owes me. He was just about to say more before I laid his ass slam out in the liquor store. I beat that nigga so bad that blood covered the dirty cheap tile of the store.

I lost my cool for a moment. I almost killed his ass for even stepping to me about Sasha. I didn't give a fuck about Sasha's past; that wasn't going to make me change how I felt about her or make me look at her differently. Just knowing where Sasha had come from really only made me want to get to know her even harder.

"Champion visitation," the woman on the intercom beeped into my four by four cell.

I climbed into the orange jumpsuit that was assigned to me and walked past the mirror to rewash my face. She clicked at the door to alert that the officer was about to come get me. They had me in a maximum-security dorm, and I was on locked down for twenty-three damn hours with six other people.

"You ready?" the white male correctional officer asked when the door popped open.

He placed the steel cold shackles on my feet, and I instantly hated the shit. I swear they were handcuffing me like I was a fucking animal. As I walked down the narrow hallway, I bypassed two doors which belonged to the medical department and staff members. The officer tried to hold a conversation with me as he took me to the small visitation room. I just mean mugged his ass because I wasn't in the mood with the fake shit today. I wasn't about to give this nigga no type of feedback. When he noticed I wasn't bothered by his ass, he shut the fuck up, and we walked in silence the rest of the way. When I stepped into the small visitation room, I took a seat in front of the bullet glass window. Once my eyes connected with Sasha, all the anger that I was feeling inside quickly evaporated. I grabbed the phone and quickly put it up to my ear.

"Hi, handsome," Sasha said as she stared into my eyes.

"Wassup, ma!" I greeted her back with a plastic smile on my face. I was happy as hell to see her ass though.

"What happened, Champ?"

"Look, I can't discuss everything here; they probably listening to what we saying," I informed her.

To be honest, I didn't give a fuck if they heard anything that I said. The only reason why I didn't want Sasha to know about what had happened and why I was behind bars was because it was only going to make her nervous and anxious. I didn't want to stress her about the Geno situation. Instead, I decided to keep what actually happened to myself. What she didn't know wouldn't hurt her. How I had laid his ass out, I doubted he came for her ever again.

"What you need me to do?" she asked with concern.

"Get my property from upfront and go back to my crib; I have some money in my room. I want you to post my bond with that."

"I will do that when I leave here."

"Hold up."

"What's wrong?" Sasha quizzed.

"I'ma call my partna so he can get the money from you, so your name won't be on my bond," I explained.

I didn't want her name to get tied up with mine. I knew she had a husband who was a lawyer, so I didn't want to bring any heat to her doorstep about the type of relationship that we had. When I broke it down to her, she understood where I was coming from. We sat there and talked about different shit until my fifteen minutes were up. She informed me that she was about to handle my business.

I caught the kiss that she threw at me in the air. Sasha was a good woman, but she belonged to someone else. That was what I hated the most. I knew in my heart that it could be any day now that she would tell me that she was through fucking around with me, and it wasn't shit that I could do about her decision. Therefore, I wasn't going to put my all into her; I was just going to keep shit neutral. I didn't want to be that lame ass nigga who fell in love with another nigga's bitch only for her to tell me she was going to work things out with her husband. I didn't want to be hurt in the end. I needed to keep my heart guarded with her. I could love her, but I wasn't about to lie to myself and fall in love with her.

As the officer escorted me back to my dorm, I noticed a strange smirk on his face. I didn't know what he thought was so funny, but instead of reading so much into his body language, I decided to think about other shit that needed my attention.

I just shook my head at him because I knew in a couple more hours, I wasn't going to have to deal with any of this shit. I was going to be back home and chilling, while his dumb fat ass would still be here working this petty ass job.

When I had made it back in my cell, I grabbed one of my favorite books titled "The Secret" by Rhonda Byne. Even though my body was locked the fuck up, the system was never going to have my mind. I always read because it always seemed to block out all the negative energy that I was feeling inside. It was my therapy and something that I did on a constant basis when I was in prison. I read Kiss Me Where It Hurts until my eyes grew heavy and sleep found me.

SASHA

Here I was, racing through traffic, trying to get to Champ's apartment. When I saw how they brought him out like an animal, I wanted nothing more than to help his ass. My heart fell to the floor just seeing him handcuffed like he was. I knew firsthand how they treated you when you got locked up. Images of back in the day began to pop back into my mind. They had me locked in my cell for so many hours, I felt as if I was about to go mad. I told myself that I was going to do my best to get his ass out and bring him home. Is it wrong for me to feel for another man? I asked myself. I knew that I wrong for fucking around with Champ and going to the jail to visit. I wasn't thinking about what would happen if someone told my husband they saw me there talking to another man. I was trying to convince myself that what I was doing was okay, but I was tired of lying to my damn self. I felt at times that the love that I showed Ryan, he didn't appreciate it, but I knew without a doubt that Champ appreciated me. The fact that he could have called anyone, but he chose to call me, let me know that Champ trusted me, and we had a bond that could not be broken.

Ring, Ring.

The sound of my phone brought me back to reality, I had gone to another planet thinking about him. When I looked down at the screen, I quickly answered.

"Hey, Ryan," I said as I pulled up at Champ's apartment complex.

"I was just calling to hear your voice."

As much as I would have wanted to hear him say that any other day, my mind was elsewhere.

"Baby, that's nice, but let me call you back," I said as I rushed him off the phone.

I told him that I loved him before I ended the call and threw the phone on the passenger seat. I stepped out my car, headed to the front door, and fumbled with his keys until I opened his door. When I stepped into Champ's crib, the smell of him filled my nose.

Damn, I thought to myself. This was really my life now. I was here, going out my way to help another nigga when I already had a husband and family at home. Never would I have ever thought that I would be doing some shit like this, but here I was.

His house was neatly organized like he always kept it. Nothing seemed to be out of place. That was another thing that I loved about Champ; he was a neat as nigga. Most men didn't believe in cleaning up or even washing a dish, but this man always had his house in check whenever I came by. Ryan, on the other hand, rarely cleaned up anything. I always was the one who was in charge of keeping the house cleaned, dishes washed, and clothes dried. He always blamed it on the fact he was always at work. I guess it was true, but damn, after a while I started to feel like I was his momma more than his wife.

I pushed the thoughts of Ryan out my mind as I began to search through his house for the money he said I would find there. When I headed into his bedroom, I pulled out his top drawer and looked under his shirts and boxers, but I didn't find any money. When my hand ran across a picture, I quickly picked it up and stared at it for a minute. It was a picture of a dark-skinned girl who I assumed was his baby mama. I knew that Champ was still crazy about his baby mama and he still loved her, even though he tried to tell me otherwise. His baby mama still had a place in his heart, and his daughter was his world.

As I stared down at the picture, the female did look familiar, but I couldn't think where I had seen the woman at. Instead of trying to rack my brain, I just tucked the picture back where I found it and opened his second drawer. I reached into the back of the drawer and grabbed a black pouch. The bag felt heavy as hell, so I assumed that I had found the bag with the money. I unzipped the pouch and poured out the contents and noticed the money that was tied in a rubber band. I counted out the amount that he needed for bail, tucked the rest of it back in the pouch, and put it back in the drawer. When Champ got out, I was going to teach him how to put his money in the bank instead of keeping it his house. I was a paranoid ass female. I never would ever keep this type of cash at my home. You never knew when someone didn't like you and decided to rob you. People were loony as hell these days, and I didn't dare trust anyone with my money. I felt safer with the banks, but even sometimes they couldn't be trusted with large sums of money.

I checked my phone and noticed it was getting late. I hurried and put the money in my purse then headed out the front door. All I had to do was wait on his friend to pull up and pick the money up from me. I was eager for him to hurry the fuck up because I was ready to see Champ again. Instead of sitting in Champ's house to wait on his homeboy to pull up, I decided to wait out in my car. As soon as I opened Champ's front door, my heart dropped.

My mouth hung open when I saw my brother Andre standing there. When Champ told me he was sending his homeboy to pick up the money from me, never would I have expected that it was going to be my baby brother.

"Sasha, what in the hell are you doing here? How in the hell do you know my homie Champ?" he asked me with confusion.

My legs grew weak, and I felt as if I was about to be sick. I could tell by how Dre was looking at me that he was ready to find out every damn thing, and there was no holding back from him.

He quickly grabbed me by my arm and pushed me down on Champ's couch.

No words were spoken for the longest time, which only made me uncomfortable.

"How long have you been fucking him?" Dre asked bluntly.

Just hearing my brother asking me something that personal really didn't sit well with me. I mean, I was a grown ass woman; there was nothing that he could tell me that I didn't already know.

I didn't say anything at first which only pissed him off.

"Sasha, your ass is married with two kids. You got a good ass husband, and here you are fucking around with a nigga who just got out of prison. Champ's like a damn brother to me, but he ain't the type of nigga you want to fall in love with, Sasha. You're way too damn good for him. Plus, he's still in love with his baby mama. Please stop whatever the fuck you are doing and go back home to your husband."

Just hearing him say all this shit really made my blood boil. I understood that Dre was my brother, but that didn't give him permission to tell me what to do with my life. I licked my lips and counted to ten before I told Dre how I really felt about him being in my personal business.

"Dre, you the best brother that a girl could ask for, but you must have forgotten that I'm the oldest. I'm grown as hell, and I know what I'm doing. Who I fuck with is not your business. I had no clue that you knew Champ, and now that I do, it still isn't going to change what Champ and I have going on." I boldly stated, walking away from him.

"Sasha!" Dre grab my wrist. " Listen to your dumbass. Have you lost yo fuckin mind? You are fucking married! Why the hell are you fucking with another nigga who can't do shit for you? Sis, you smarter than that shit. You can't put your marriage in jeopardy for Champ. Think about your two kids and what they will think if Ryan and them find out what you are doing."

My heart was racing, and I wanted nothing more than to punch Dre in the face.

"All I'm asking you to do is leave my homie alone and be a wife and a mother to them kids you got by your husband. Whatever you and your hubby got going on, you need to work that shit out, because playing 'round here in these streets ain't going to do nothing but get your heart broke."

I bit my tongue and rolled my eyes before I stood up to grab the money out my purse.

"Here is the money to get Champ out of jail."

Dre snatched the money from my hand and put it in his back pocket. The ringing of my phone sent my ass in overdrive. My eyes lit up when I noticed it was Champ calling me from the county jail. I guess Dre must have known who it was just by watching me, because time I tried to pick up, he snatched the phone from my hand and threw that bitch to the wall.

I covered my mouth as I ran to pick up my phone which was now rocking a cracked screen. I was beyond pissed off and was ready to fuck Dre's ass up. He had gone too damn far.

"Sis, you must think I'm playing with your ass? Leave Champ alone," he spat at me.

I looked up at Dre and didn't hesitate to smack his ass.

"You must ain't heard shit that I fucking said, nigga. I ain't leaving him alone. Move along and stay out my damn business."

I grabbed my cracked phone and threw it in my purse. I was almost out the door when Dre called out my name, but I ignored his ass. Instead, I headed out the door and jumped in my car.

CHAMP

THE NEXT DAY

"You aren't gone yet?" CJ asked as he shook the bars to his cell.

"Not yet; in a couple more hours, I will be out this bitch," I ensured him.

CJ was a nigga that had come back to Lee County because he was getting his case reheard. Since his cell was across from mine, he and I had been getting to know one another. I had learned that he was locked up for armed robbery, a crime he said he didn't actually do. What I found stupid was he didn't rob the bank himself. He just was the nigga who was driving the getaway car. The fact that no one could point him at the scene of the crime as the one actually robbing the bank made the case a little challenging for the D.A. to accuse him of such a hideous crime.

"What kind of work you do?" CJ asked curiously.

"I'm a personal trainer. Matter fact, the girl that came to see me is one of the girls I train."

CJ stared at me with a perplexed expression on his face.

"So, you were training your girl?"

"She's not my girl, just a really good friend."

"Bruh, I been locked up for a minute, but y'all ain't just friends," he mumbled.

"Why you say that?"

"From what I seen from my side of the room, she was near tears when they brought her ass out to visitation," he explained.

"I'm telling you, nigga, we just friends. She's married anyway."

"She might have his ring on, but you got her heart, Bruh, but that's just what I think. I could be wrong, but rarely am I ever wrong about a female."

I laid back on my mattress and began to meditate on our conversation. Do I have Sasha's heart? I asked myself.

Even when I tried not thinking about her, I found myself thinking about her more than ever. If it was true, there was no way that she and I would ever be able to be together because she was married with kids. She had a family, and I wasn't the type of nigga to break up a happy home. But even though I didn't want to break up her marriage, I still couldn't stop thinking about what happened if she decided to leave her man. I smiled as I thought back to the night her and I finally took it too far and slept together.

"Mmmm... Yessss, Champ!" she screamed as I rammed my dick inside of her.

She looked back at me and bit down on her lower lip just before she started to throw it on a nigga. That shit fucked my whole mind up. The more she fucked me, the more I grinded my dick inside her guts. When I grabbed the back of her neck, she moaned out my name. I could tell her ass was turned the fuck on because her pussy was leaking her juices.

"Damn this dick good!" Sasha cried out as I continued to pound inside her.

"Champion, standby for medical," the woman on the intercom stated, which snapped me out of the sex session that Sasha and I had shared. I hit the button on the intercom, making sure she had the right name. Only thing I was on standby for was to get the fuck out of there and head home. I pulled back on my jumpsuit, washed my face, and waited until the guard came to get me.

"You ready?" Officer Clark asked.

I came to the front of the cell and nodded my head to let him know I was ready to head out. Within seconds, my door clicked open and I took a deep breath. I was ready to get the fuck out of here, and still there was no word from Sasha on if she had gotten hold of my money. Officer Clark handcuffed me, and as I followed him out my cell, I noticed CJ sitting down in his cell, writing a letter. I assumed it was to his girlfriend. When our eyes met, we both nodded at one another in respect.

As we neared the end of the hallway, I asked Officer Clark for a phone call because I wanted to check on my bail.

"Alright, I will check on it for you," he explained as he opened the door for me.

"If you come through, I will make sure to put you on to a bad bitch when I get out of here," I convinced him.

Officer Clark's eyes began to shine with amusement.

After we entered through the double doors, the medical room was located on the left side of the hallway. The medical room was small and only included a medium-sized stretcher, a wooden desk, and a scale. When I stepped inside, a plus size nurse was sitting down in a chair waiting on me.

She nodded her head at me before pointing to the plastic blue chair that was in front of her. I sighed with frustration but took a seat where she directed me to. She took my vitals and heart rate as Officer Clark stood watch.

"Clark, you going to check on that phone call?"

"Yeah, as soon as she…"

"Clark gone head and handle that. I will watch him while you gone." The nurse said to the officer.

He released me then went down the hall. She looked back at me then started smiling. What messed me up was when she closed the door.

"So, you the one I've been hearing so much about," she muttered as she began to palm my dick. I couldn't really move because my wrist and feet were in shackles. I swear I felt defenseless.

"Hold up."

I squirmed in my seat, but she wasn't having any of that shit. The more I tried to resist her from getting to my dick, the more aggressive she got. It wasn't long before she found exactly what she was looking for and planted it right in her mouth.

"Mmm, they didn't lie about you at all," she moaned as she sucked on the tip of my dick. As much as I wanted her to stop what she was doing, it was time that I was honest with myself and accept the fact that I was enjoying the pressure she was putting on my dick. Instead of fighting with her, I decided to leave that shit alone and let her do what she had to do, because there wasn't shit that I could do about it anyway. She briefly pulled my dick from her mouth and spit on it before she slid me back into her hungry mouth. She gave me one last suck before I shot my cum into her mouth. I was in utter shock. I couldn't believe what had just occurred. She wiped her mouth then winked at me. Officer Clark opened the door a few moments later and said he had gotten everything lined up for me to use the phone.

I had just been slick raped and was ready to get the fuck up out of there since Clark had gotten the phone situation handled.

"Have a nice day, Champion," the nurse said while touching my shoulder.

Officer Clark grabbed me by my arm and escorted me through the double doors toward the intake area. It was so stink that I was close to vomiting my lunch that I had eaten only an hour earlier. When I looked to my left, I noticed there were two dudes in the cell fussing about some crazy shit. One of the niggas looked familiar, but I couldn't remember where I knew him from. Officer Clark let one of my hands go free as I picked up the phone and dialed my homeboy's number. He picked up, but I could barely hear him over the loud noise in the background.

"Hello!" I yelled out over the background noise.

"Yeah! What up, partna?" Dre said drily.

"Dre, did you get the money? Hurry up and come get me, nigga. I'm about to go crazy in this bitch."

"I'm on my way, Bruh," Dre muttered into the phone.

I hung up the phone, and Officer Clark handcuffed my hands back together and escorted me back to my cell.

As I laid in my bunk, I could sense something wasn't right with Dre. He was talking all dry and shit like something was bothering him. I shook my head because whatever had him in his feelings, I knew he was going to let a nigga know what it was when he came to scoop my ass up.

SASHA

Tears fell from my face, and rage was filling a deep hole that was in my heart. I couldn't believe that my brother Andre was the nigga who I was expecting to come pick up the money. I was still upset with how shit had gone down with my brother and me. When Andre found out that I was the one that was fucking around with Champ, things didn't go too well. The fact that this nigga had gotten angry and had fucked up my phone was what really hurt me. Andre had lost his fucking mind. He must had forgotten that I was the oldest.

He had no right to tell me who I could talk to. He wasn't my fucking daddy, and it was time that he realized that shit.

I cared about Champ with all my heart. When I was around him, he made me feel free. He listened to all my issues and was always concerned about me and my feelings. I felt like if I didn't have a husband and kids at home, Champ and I could be so much more then friends. My heart craved his companionship, but I knew deep down inside I wasn't going to have that, at least not right now.

I was tired and frustrated that I had to wait over three hours to get another iPhone. I was still pissed off at Andre but decided to let the shit go. I had a new phone, but I was still angry this nigga had fucked up my first one. I was just about to leave Verizon Wireless when my new iPhone began to ring. I groaned when I noticed Ryan's name flashing across the screen.

"Yes," I said into the phone as I hit accept on my phone.

"How long is it gonna be before you get home?" Ryan asked.

Lately, he had been coming home early and had been pressing me to spend time with him. I had gotten so used to him not being around and not having time to do shit with me, I wasn't really interested in spending time with him anymore. He was just a few months too late. I wished he would have been doing this a few months ago, but he was too engrossed with his work.

"I will be home in a minute. I'm heading over to Sweet Pea's house for a quick minute," I mumbled into the phone.

A few moments later, I turned on to Sweet Pea's street and pulled up at her crib. I had to talk to her about what I was going through. She was the only friend that I had that I trusted.

"Okay, baby, I will be waiting on you," Ryan softly said into the phone before disconnecting the call.

I slid my phone back in my purse just before I pulled into Sweet Pea's driveway. I noticed her car wasn't there and figured that Rodney was out joy riding in her shit. Glancing at the clock, I knew she was probably sitting on her couch watching Law and Order. When I stepped out, a mist of sour air invaded my nostrils. I didn't know what that smell was coming from, but it had me feeling like I wanted to throw up my breakfast. I hit the alarm on my car and headed to Sweet Pea's porch. Beer bottles laid all over the porch from where Rodney probably had been drinking outside. I shook my head at the mess. Sweet Pea could do so much better. I still couldn't wrap my mind around why the fuck she dealt with Rodney's nasty ass.

I opened the screen door then softly knocked about three times as I waited for her to answer the door. When I heard the door unlock, I slid my phone back into my purse and came face to face with Rodney. When the door opened, the awful smell hit my ass in the face yet again. I quickly turned my nose up and stepped back from Rodney.

"Wassup?" Rodney asked with a devilish smirk on his face.

"Is Sweet Pea here?"

"She at work," he stated as he rubbed his chest.

I cringed inside when I noticed this nigga didn't have a shirt on and was dressed in a pair of basketball shorts that looked dingy and dirty.

"I thought she was off today?"

"Naw, she got another job working in Leesburg," he informed me as he opened the screen door wider.

I didn't respond because I didn't even know that Sweet Pea had even gotten another job. I was pissed the fuck off that he had her out working two jobs when his sorry ass could have gotten a job instead. I wanted to get the fuck out of there because being around Rodney's stinking ass was beginning to give me the creeps.

I grabbed my keys out my purse and was heading to my car, when Rodney called out my name.

"Sasha, somebody told me to deliver you a message," he said as he rubbed his hands together.

I just stared at him. I had no clue what he was about to say, but my heart told me it was about to be some shit I didn't like.

"Geno told me to tell you that your time is running out."

Even though I was scared as fuck, I didn't let Rodney see the fear in my eyes.

"Fuck you and Geno!" I yelled before I jumped in my car and sped away in a rage.

I couldn't believe this shit was happening to me. First Champ gets locked up, then I get into it with Andre, and now Geno was sending me messages and shit. I had way too much shit going at the moment, and I felt as if I was about to lose my mind. I needed a drink to calm my nerves, so I quickly headed over to Travis's Bar and Grill. Since it was only noon, it wasn't packed as it normally be late at night.

As I headed inside, I noticed that Travis had upgraded. Back when I was coming on the regular, there was only one pool table, and now it was several. The furniture had been remodeled and everything had been repainted. Music blasted in the distance as I walked over to the bar, took a seat, and ordered a shot of Patrón. As I sipped on my drink, I couldn't think about anyone else but Champ. I just prayed that he was okay. I so desperately wanted to talk to him, but in due time, Champ would be coming back home.

The more Patrón I sipped, the angrier and frustrated I became. I stood up and almost lost my balance. I was tipsy but not wasted. Instead of trying to leave right then, I sat back down. The room felt as if it was spinning, and that's when I realized I had went over the limit of my alcohol intake. I looked down at the empty glasses and noticed I had over five empty glasses looking back at me. At least I thought it was five. I was too damn drunk to even count straight. I tried to stand up yet again, but it was an epic fail. I fell straight to the ground and everything went black.

AN HOUR LATER

"Sasha."

I groaned in pain when I heard someone calling out my name. I opened my eyes and could have sworn I saw Champ looking down at me.

"Cha…" Just when my blurry vision came into focus, that's when I noticed Ryan staring at me, and I was in my bedroom. I sat up in bed and rubbed my hands through my messy hair.

"Sasha, what is going on with you?" Ryan asked, staring into my eyes.

"I'm just dealing with a lot of shit right about now."

"Baby, talk to me. What are you dealing with? Do you know how scared I got when Travis called me to tell me that you had passed out? I came as soon as I could and brought you home. Never have you done anything like this. Please, love, tell me what is going on with you. You got a nigga worried. I don't know what I would do if something ever happened to you."

I bit down on my bottom lip as I tried to think of a lie. I didn't want him to know the real reason I had been acting all strange.

"Sweet Pea having family problems, and I've been trying to be there for her," I lied.

"Baby, that's all? Is this what got you acting strange and weird lately? You aren't acting yourself at all. I don't ever want you to think that you can't talk to me about what is bothering you. I'm your husband," he said with compassion in his voice.

I licked my lips before a single tear fell from my cheeks.

"That's all that's wrong with me, baby. I'm just worried about Sweet Pea. She's like a sister to me."

I ran my hand across his face to reassure him that nothing else was bothering me.

"I love you, Sasha," Ryan confessed.

Hearing him say those words made me feel horrible inside. He grabbed my hand and stared at me. I felt this nigga was looking into my soul.

"Well, when you hear what I have to say, I think it will cheer you up. I have some good news to share with you," Ryan said with a smile on his face.

"I'm listening."

"I'm running for the position as a Magistrate Judge," he said with excitement in his voice.

"Congratulations, baby," I said, kissing him on his soft lips.

He brushed my hair from my face before he then kissed me once more. I pushed back from him, and he quickly asked if I was okay yet again.

"We need to talk. It's something I got to tell you," I told him seriously.

I couldn't take the lies any longer; it was time that Ryan knew the truth.

"I, I…"

He cut me off before placing his fingers on my lips

"Tell me later, baby. I just want to make love to my beautiful wife."

He leaned me back and threw his tongue in my mouth. I wanted to pull away, to tell him to get off m, but I was too weak to fight with him. Instead, I laid back like he demanded and decided to let him have his way with me. I wanted nothing more than to tell him that I had been cheating on him with another man, and just when I had finally gotten the courage to give him the truth, he had cut me off. In my mind, I wanted to scream out what I was feeling, but instead, I tucked my emotions away and closed my eyes. As Ryan's lips trailed up and down my body, not once did my pussy get wet for him.

I just wasn't in the mood to fuck, but apparently, Ryan was. I squeezed my eyes shut as he pulled my panties to the side and began to lick and suck on my clit. I opened my eyes rather quickly when he pulled his hard dick out and began to play with my pussy.

I cried out and gripped the sheets as he slid my panties off my ass and slid his dick into my pussy. I was wet enough for him to stick it in, but that was about it. The sex was dry and uninteresting for me. My mind was somewhere else. I had so much that I was thinking about that I wasn't even aroused with fucking my husband. His loud moans in my ear was letting me know he was enjoying himself, but he had no clue that I was silently praying that he would hurry up, bust his nut, and get off of me. I lay there as he slid in and out of me, before he pulled out of me and flipped me over on my stomach. I squeezed my eyes shut as he sucked on my neck before he entered me from the back. I pretended to enjoy his penetration, even though the only man I wanted inside me was Champ. I was relieved when he caught his nut and rolled off me. Instead of laying around and doing some pillow talk like I used to do, I quickly hurried to the bathroom so I could wash the scent of him from me. As I showered, and as the water poured down on my body, I began to wonder if staying in this marriage was even worth it.

CHAMP

I hurried to collect my belongings because I was ready to get out this hellhole. All I could think about was Faith and praying that Trina hadn't done anything crazy. I tried calling Trina's phone but got no answer. I began to wonder where Dre and Sasha were at. They both weren't answering their phone. I already knew that Dre had probably pushed up on Sasha, but I had no clue if Sasha was down to fuck around with my homeboy behind my back or not. One thing I knew about a married woman was, if she wasn't loyal to her husband, there was no way she was going to be loyal to any other nigga. Sasha was a cool, down to earth chick, but at the end of the day, I didn't know her well enough to know if she would fuck around with another nigga behind my back.

I didn't hesitate to bust through the double doors toward my freedom. I was ready to head home and take me a long hot shower and chill. When the sun hit my face, I knew the horrible nightmare had ended. I was free yet again. My eyes took in my surroundings, and that's when I noticed Dre's ruby red Chevy right in front of me. Dre stepped out as I walked over to the car and dapped me up.

"Wassup, Bruh?"

"Shit, I just been grinding."

"Dats the move. What happened to you after you picked the money up from Sasha?" I questioned.

I was trying to figure out what Dre had going on because, in my mind, he was trying to push up on her by how strange he was acting.

"I had some family issues that came up that I had to handle," he said as he opened his door.

I hopped in on the passenger side and closed the door behind me.

When I sat down, I noticed a liquor bottle below my feet. I quickly grabbed it and noticed it was halfway empty. I stared at Dre and shook my head. It was way too early in the day for him to already had killed half a bottle of vodka. I pulled out my phone so I could try to text Sasha and Trina to let them know that I was about to swing by.

"You must be trying to check up on your Shawty?" Dre asked coldly.

"Naw, I'm trying to get up with Trina on some important shit."

"So, what's up with you and Trina?"

"Nothing; the same ole shit."

"Y'all ain't talking about working it out?"

"That would be nice, but she got too much going on right now. Right before I got locked up, Faith told me in the car that she was planning on moving to Boston."

We talked for the next half hour before we pulled up at my crib. He listened as I told him about Geno and how I wanted to fuck his ass up. Dre didn't speak, just listened, which I found very strange. Something was up with Dre, and I had no clue what it was. We hopped out the car and headed to my front door. I looked back at Dre and asked him was he good.

"I just need to talk to you about something. It's been on my mind real heavy. It's about that girl you sent me to pick up the money from."

"You mean Sasha?"

"Yeah, her."

"What about her?" I asked suspiciously.

This was the moment that I had been waiting for. I was curious to know what actually went down after he got the money from her.

"She's my older sister, Bruh."

I was speechless. There were no words that I could form to even reply to what he had just told me.

I thought this nigga was playing, but when I looked at him, he had a serious expression on his face.

"Damn, it's a small world," I stated as I tried to go back to unlocking the door.

Dre and I had been cool as fuck growing up. We were always getting into some shit together. Yet, there was never a time that I had met his sister. I didn't know nothing about her and had never even seen a picture of her. Back in the day when Dre and I was running the streets, he and I barely ever went to his house; we always met at my crib or met up in the streets. Yes, I knew he had an older sister, but I never thought that I was going to one day be smashing her ass and not know who in the hell she was. Every time I came over when we were growing up, his sister was never around; she was out and about. Damn, if I would have known that Sasha knew Dre, there was no way in hell I would have ever fucked around with her. But it was too damn late now; the deed had been done.

Dre grabbed my shoulder just when I was about to step into my apartment.

"I need for you to stop seeing her."

I noticed that his fist was tightly closed, and he looked like he was pissed the fuck off.

"What you mean stop seeing her?" I asked him.

"Bruh, I'm serious. Stay away from my damn sister," he said aggressively.

I saw the pain in his eyes. I grabbed the bottom of my chin then took a deep breath.

"Aight, Bruh. I won't see her again."

Even though Sasha and I had gotten close, I had been knowing Dre over a decade. I wasn't about to let no woman come between our friendship.

Dre nodded his head and un-balled his fist.

We gave each other dap, and I offered him a quick drink, but he immediately told me that he had to go handle some street business.

Even though I didn't want to get back in the street life, I asked him if he knew where I could get me a gun. He quickly told me that wasn't going to be a problem, and he would get one for me. There was no way I was about to let Geno catch me slipping ever again. As I headed into the kitchen to pour me a drink, all I could think about was how I was going to tell Sasha that she and I were going to have to leave one another alone.

I swallowed my first glass of vodka and headed toward the bathroom so I could hop in the shower. I stood under the water trying to make sense of things. My thoughts were everywhere, but my mind heavily rested on Trina and Faith. I still didn't know why Trina wanted to move all the way to Boston. As the hot water hit my body, I heard an urgent knock on my front door. I quickly turned off the shower and prayed that it was Trina coming to enlighten me about moving out of Georgia. I dried my body off before grabbing a pair of sweatpants and heading toward the door. As I made my way to the door, the knocking became louder.

"I'm coming!" I yelled out.

When I turned the knob, I nearly fell over. I wasn't expecting to see my brother standing on my doorstep.

"Jerome!" I said with emotions.

"Elijah, I need you, Bruh."

I watched him as he wiped the sweat from his face.

"What you need, Bruh? You know I got you."

"I fucked up, bro."

When I heard them words, I knew something wasn't right. There had never been a time that Jerome had told me that he had fucked up.

"What you do, Bruh?"

"I put my hands on Karen. I beat her bad, bro," he confessed, looking at the ground.

I moved aside as I let my brother come inside. Jerome took a seat on the couch, with a blank expression on his face. I took a seat on the other couch and waited for him to tell me what had happened.

I wasn't a saint, but I wasn't a fan about a man hitting a woman. When he told me that his wife was cheating on him with someone on her job, I understood why he had lost his temper. I quickly tried to tell him that things were going to be okay, but I could tell that his mind was somewhere else. He looked down at his watch and stood up.

"Elijah, I got to turn myself in," he said, handing me a white card. "Get in contact with him and tell him who you are."

I just nodded to let him know I would do whatever it was he wanted me to do.

"What about Jade and Tiffany?" I asked as his hands grabbed the knob to the door.

Tears fell from his eyes and his knees hit the carpet.

"Jay, hold it together," I said as I helped him up.

His family was his whole world, and losing them wasn't something my brother was ever going to get over.

"I got you, Bruh." I had to be here for him because when I needed him, he would stop and be by my side until I got my shit together. It was only right I returned the favor.

"Let me throw on some clothes," I said as I headed toward my room.

I looked at my brother differently after I dropped him off to the police station to turn himself in for beating the shit out of his wife. I had nothing but mad respect for my brother because there was no way I would have ever turned myself in. I still couldn't believe that my whole world was falling apart right in front of my eyes. The more I tried to shake it off, the more I felt my life was being sucked out of me. Jerome had suggested that Jada and Tiffany stayed with me until things got settled down. He didn't want Karen's family to be saying no crazy shit to his kids while he was away. I didn't have a problem with keeping my nieces; family was everything to me.

I tried calling Trina so I could go by and scoop up Faith so she could play with her cousins, but I got no answer. I was super irritated because I hadn't heard from anything from Trina or my daughter since I'd been out. I had left several messages on her voicemail and still had not heard back from her. In the back of my mind, I was trying to talk myself out of coming out of character and acting a damn fool.

After I had pulled off from dropping my brother off, I noticed that I had a few missed calls from Yolanda. I ignored them all, because I blamed her for why I had gone to jail in the first place. She was messaging me, begging me to come by her house, and after she kept on blowing up my phone, I finally shot her a message, declining her offer of coming by her crib. When she told me that I wasn't her only nigga, that was when she fucked up. There was no way I was about to get into it with a lame ass nigga about a bitch. I learned from Trina that sometimes forever wasn't forever. That was why I never gave these females my heart. I knew they couldn't be trusted.

Sasha was a good woman, but she wasn't the type of woman that I was looking for. I didn't want to put all my feelings into her, because she was still married, and she was never going to be mine. Now as I sat back and thought about the warning from Dre, I figured everything had worked out for the best. Why fuck with his sister and break up a happy home when I could smash any bitch that I wanted who was single, who didn't have a husband and kids waiting on her at home? I had already made up my mind that as soon as Sasha and I saw one another, that she and I were going to dead our friendship. It wasn't going to lead to anything but tears and a broken heart.

What He Don't Know Won't Hurt

I couldn't stop thinking about Jerome. I knew he was hurting. I understood how it felt to love someone so hard only to find out they had betrayed you. That was a very hurtful feeling. I could remember when I first cheated on Trina. She nutted up on a nigga, and she just was a girlfriend. Just imagine what a wife and husband would do when they found out the other had been unfaithful. Husband and wife was a huge title to rock, and both parties had to be sure they were ready for the good and hard times. That was why I was waiting until the right woman came along before I got married. I wanted to make sure I was on my grown man shit before I said the words 'I Do.'

I had just pulled up at the spot that Jerome told me to go to, to get him help after he turned himself in. As soon as I walked through the double doors, I wanted nothing more than to turn my ass back around when I spotted Roshika hanging up the phone.

"Shit," I mumbled to myself as I walked over to where she was sitting behind the desk.

"Damn, nigga. You don't know a bitch no Mo'?" Roshika asked.

If this wouldn't have been for my brother, I would have dipped the fuck out. I wasn't in the mood to deal with this bitch.

All I wanted to do was talk to this dude that was on the card my brother gave me. I pulled out the business card that Jerome had given me just before he turned himself in.

"What type of shit have you gotten yourself into?"

"Why does it matter to you?" I asked her with irritation in my voice.

I took a deep breath so I wouldn't snap on this bitch and hurt her feelings.

"Roshika, we can have this discussion later. All I want you to do is do me this one favor so I can get my brother out of trouble," I said angrily while hitting my hand on the counter to get her attention.

"So are you going to help me or not?"

"Mmmm… I love seeing you like this," she flirted.

I was just about to say some shit to hurt her feelings because I really wasn't in the mood for her games, but I clamped my mouth shut when she picked up the phone and told the dude that he had a visitor. After she had confirmed that he was going to be out shortly, she told me that I owed her. I pulled her out some cash and was about to hand it to her ass, but she quickly told me she didn't want my money.

"I want some of that dick again."

"I don't know about that," I replied truthfully.

Last time I had fucked around with her and had given her some dick, she started acting crazier than a muthafucka.

"Just dick me down one more time. After that, I will leave you alone," she begged.

"When I get everything situated, I will give you a call."

"I'm for real, Champ."

"You got my word."

When I heard the door click, I knew it had to be the dude that Jerome wanted me to talk to.

Roshika introduced me to the dude and quickly got back to work. I shook his hand and mentioned Jerome's name.

"My brother wanted me to come holla at you."

"Has he gotten himself into trouble?"

I explained to him what my brother's situation was, and he quickly hit the counter.

"Damn," he mumbled.

"As soon as I finish up in here, I will head over to the county jail to check on him," he said.

I thanked him before we shook hands.

"Your brother and I are good friends. I told him I was here if he ever need something."

"Thank you for that, but I got a question."

"What you want to know?"

"Do you think you can help me with my situation as well? I sort of got into a fight with some nigga at the store and ended up getting locked up at the Lee County Jail."

He assured me that he was going to make a few phone calls to get the problem handled. I gave him one of my cards with my name on it so he would have my contact information to reach me.

He tapped my card before sticking it into his pocket.

"I will be in touch, and by the way, my name is Ryan. It was good to meet you."

SASHA

I had just woken up while Ryan was still snoring next to me. I shook him lightly to let him know that it was time to get up. I hurried to the bathroom to relieve myself and washed my face. Just when I was about to hop in the shower, Ryan grabbed me and placed a kiss on my neck. His dick was pressed up against my naked body, but I wasn't in the mood to entertain him with no sex. I had too many things running through my mind, and having sex with him wasn't on my list.

I moved away from him, and I guess Ryan understood I wasn't in the mood.

"What your plans for today?" Ryan asked.

"Well, I got to stop by the kids' school and then stop by Verizon so they can take a look at this phone. This phone got a mind of its on."

As the hot water poured down my naked body, I felt nothing but relief. As I showered, Ryan yelled out that he was going to try to get off early later that night.

"Since the election is about to begin, I'm going to soon be at the office a lot more then I normally am. I just want to spend as much time with you as I can," Ryan said loudly.

All I truly wanted to do was enjoy my shower. What Ryan was talking about wasn't anything but bullshit. I wasn't about to get my hopes up about him getting off work early, and I damn sure didn't care about it.

"Baby, you need to be heading to work before you be late. You know you hate being late," I told him truthfully.

I stepped out the shower and was drying my body off.

"I know, baby. I'm about to leave now, but be ready when I get home. I'm going to beat that pussy up."

I rolled my eyes because I highly doubted his ass came home to beat anything up, especially with him running for magistrate judge. Instead of telling him what I truthfully felt,

I smiled in his face and watched as he walked out the bathroom.

After Ryan had left, I hurried to get dressed and headed to Malcolm's room first and then Ashanti's room so I could get them up for school. Within an hour, they were both up and dressed. We headed out the house in record time. After dropping both the kids off to school, I wanted nothing more than to drop by Champ's house to see what he was doing. I had tossed and turned all night long because I was craving this touch. I pulled out my phone as soon as I pulled up at Verizon and shot Champ and Sweet Pea a message.

ME: Good morning Champ. I been thinking about you all night. Hit me up when you get this because I'm worried about you.

ME: Sweet Pea call me ASAP

After stepping out the car and waiting in line for over thirty minutes, I finally got a chance to speak to someone about my phone. This phone was brand new, and it already was giving me problems. I waited patiently for them to factory reset my phone and sweep it clean. After leaving Verizon, I looked at the time and noticed that I had to hurry my ass up to get to Malcolm's meeting, but I quickly took a detour and headed to Champ's house instead. I just couldn't get this nigga off my damn brain. I had to see him, and I didn't really care at the moment about anything else. I always attended my kids' meetings, so I figured I was allowed to miss at least one.

I was halfway to Champ's crib when my phone began to ring. I pulled my phone out my purse and groaned when I noticed Ryan's name on the screen. I picked up, even though I didn't want to.

"Hey," I said into the phone as I turned down my stereo.

"Aye, beautiful. What time you are leaving the house to head to the meeting?"

"I'm on the way to the kid's school now," I lied.

"Everything good? I asked curiously.

"Yes, baby, I'm good. When you leave the school, make sure you come by the office; you and I can have lunch together."

"Damn, baby, I wish I could join you, but I promised Sweet Pea that I was going to have lunch with her. I'm sorry, baby."

"It's all good, baby. I will just see you tonight."

"Yeah, that's fine also. I promise to give you some tonight."

"I can't wait," he said into the phone before disconnecting the call.

When I hung up the phone, I shook my head. "Damn, I am getting real good at this lying," I said to myself.

I called Sweet Pea up to let her know what all she had been missing with my drama filled life. After I had told her about what was going on with me, she quickly began to tell me about this nigga she was fucking with. She claimed she was really feeling this nigga. She was talking about this nigga so hard that I almost missed my turn. When I pulled up at Champ's spot, I ended my call with Sweet Pea. I spotted Champ's two cars which let me know that he was indeed home. I said a silent prayer before stepping out my car and heading toward Champ's front porch. My heart was pumping loudly against my chest as I waited for him to come to the door. When his door swung open, my knees grew weak when I noticed him standing in front of me. He was looking good as hell, with his white wife beater and gray basketball shorts. I quickly grabbed hold of him and didn't dare let him go.

"I'm so glad that you are okay."

Yeah, I'm Gucci, Sasha," Champ said while hugging me back.

His whole body was smelling good as hell which only made my pussy wetter.

He pulled away from me first, which I found strange.

"Sasha, I need to talk to you about something," he said in a sad tone.

What's wrong, baby?" I asked.

"Sasha, you a wonderful person and all, but we can't do this anymore." His words cut me right in the heart.

"Why, baby?" I asked him with tears in my eyes.

I tried touching him, but he quickly brushed my hands away from him.

"You're married, Sasha, and your Dre's sister."

"And?"

"I told him that I would leave you the hell alone out of respect."

"I'm not trying to hear that shit, Champ."

"We got brotherhood, that's why."

He tried walking away, but I jumped in his way.

"Since you have been in my life, you have changed my whole vision of things. Yes, I'm married, but I'm not happy with him. When I lay in bed, you are the one I think about."

"I'm sorry, Sasha, but I gave your brother my word."

"I guess Andre was right about you," I said as I headed to the door.

"What did he say about me?" Champ asked.

"He told me that you don't care about anyone or their feelings. The only person you care about is yourself."

"That's not true."

"If you say so."

I grabbed the doorknob and was just about to walk out. I was frustrated as hell and was ready to get the hell away from him.

"Sasha! Wait."

I turned around and stared into his eyes.

"I care about you dearly, I can't deny that, but no matter how much I care or want to be with you at that, at the end of the day, you could never be mine fully because of that ring on your finger," he said.

"I wear his ring, but my heart belongs to you."

Champ was about to speak, but I cut him off when I slid my tongue down his throat. There was no way in hell I was about to let my little brother ruin what Champ and I had. I was a grown ass woman and was old enough to make my own decisions. We kissed passionately as I caressed his chest, just before I ripped his wife beater off his body. He grabbed my ass which made me moan into his neck. He picked me up and carried me to his bedroom, where he and I hurried and undressed.

He stroked his rock-hard dick just before he pushed me down on the bed and slid into me from the back. I pushed my face down into the pillow as he gripped my hips and began to fill my pussy up with his thick dick. I cried and screamed out his name as I gripped the bed sheets.

He smacked my ass a few times just before he told me he was about to bust his nut. I screamed out as he slammed into me for the last time and spilled his seed inside me.

*****

After leaving Champ's apartment, I felt nothing but relief. All the issues I had were gone, and I felt that he and I could get through anything. He put that dick on me so good that I almost forgot I had a husband and kids at home. My pussy was still trembling from his touch. He knew exactly what to do to please my body, and he knew all the right things to say to melt my heart.

I was so much in my fantasy world that I had no clue that it was late until I pulled up at my crib and noticed that the school bus was arriving the same time I was. I groaned when I noticed that Ryan was already home as well. I was still in utter disbelief because rarely did Ryan ever keep his word about coming home early. I got out the car and headed inside to find Ryan was cooking.

Within an hour, all of us were sitting at the dinner table enjoying our dinner. I could barely eat because my pussy was still aching between my legs. The dinner was good, and the fact that he had gone all out his way to cook was the only reason why I kept a smile on my face and tried to eat.

"Aye, Mom!" Malcolm snapped at me.

Malcolm had brought me back to Earth because I was on another planet.

I looked up and noticed that my son was staring over at me.

"My teacher told me to tell you since you missed the meeting..."

When those words came out Malcolm's mouth, I wanted nothing more than to die.

Ryan dropped his fork and turned his attention to me. As Malcolm explained what his teacher told him to tell me, I could imagine the questions that Ryan was bound to start asking me.

My heart was beating a mile a minute. Instead of me trying to explain myself to Ryan, I just kept my eyes on Malcolm.

CHAMP

I was on my way to pick Faith up from school when I decided to hit Jerome's lawyer up to see why his bail hadn't been issued yet. Jerome's lawyer told me that he was working on filing for a motion. When his lawyer told me that the judge felt like Jerome was a threat to society, I knew that the court system was going to take a bitch's side over the nigga's. Jerome's lawyer seemed like he was a pretty cool guy; only thing that kind of made me uncomfortable was he was the type of nigga that was way too damn affectionate. I wasn't with all that hugging and shit, but overall, besides that, he was cool people.

"Hey, Daddy!" Faith screamed as she hopped out her chair and ran toward me.

I hadn't really gotten the chance to spend time with Faith like I wanted, so I decided that today would make a good day to pick her up and spend some father/daughter time together.

"How my angel doing?" I asked her, gently giving her a warm hug.

"I'm doing good, Daddy," she said as she reached into her book bag. "Guess what, Daddy?"

"What, baby girl?"

"I got a leading role in the school's Christmas play," she said, showing me the flyer.

"I am so proud of you, baby girl."

I kissed her on the forehead then gave her a high five.

"This calls for something special."

Her face lit up.

"Pizza, Daddy, please."

I should've known that her favorite food was pizza. Faith would eat pizza for breakfast, lunch, and dinner.

"Anything for you, baby," I said as I turned around and signed her out.

Her teacher passed me a few of Faith's papers that I signed and gave back to her. I grabbed Faith by her hand and we headed out the door.

When we stepped out the door, I wasn't expecting to see Trina posted up on her car with her hands folded.

Faith ran toward Trina with her Christmas flyer in her hand, but Trina didn't pay her any mind. Instead, she was eye balling my ass like she wanted to say some foul shit.

This was the first time that we were able to be face to face, and I wanted nothing more than to get to the bottom of her moving back to Boston. I watched as Trina grabbed Faith and put her in the back. Right before Trina opened the driver's door, I grabbed her by the arm.

"Trina, hold up. We need to talk."

"About what?"

"You moving to Boston."

"There is nothing for us to talk about. I made a decision, and I'm not changing that, Elijah.

She knew exactly what to do and say to push my button. She knew I hated my government name.

"Why Boston, Trina?" I asked as I held on to the driver's door.

"Look, I know it seems crazy, but this is something that I have to do."

"I don't wanna fuss with you, Trina. Just make sure to bring Faith to my crib later on."

She squinted her eyes at me like I was speaking in a foreign language.

"I'm going to have Jade and Tiffany with me for a while, so I wanted Faith to come over so she can play with her cousins, and I promised Faith pizza. I try my best to keep my word."

"Since when?" Trina shot at me."

"Since now, so get out your feelings and bring Faith over later. It can be a family event."

Trina rolled her eyes before finally telling me that she would bring Faith by later that day.

"You lucky it's the weekend, but we can't stay for too long," Trina said seriously.

"That's fine with me," I said as I removed my hand from her door to let her get in her car.

"I appreciate it."

"Whatever, nigga," she mumbled before hopping in her car and driving off.

FOUR HOURS LATER

I was sitting on the couch, looking at the clock on the wall, while I waited for Trina to pull up with Faith. I was beginning to get furious because it was getting late, and Trina still was nowhere to be seen. All I wanted to do was spend time with Faith before she had to leave, and Trina couldn't even let me do that without her getting in her feelings. Jade and Tiffany were in the back playing with her toys and waiting patiently for Faith to arrive. Tomorrow morning, they were going back home to their grandma's house, so even their time with me was limited.

Karen had called me last night to let me know that she had gotten out of the hospital and she was feeling a lot better. She also told me that she was going to go back to stay with her mother for a few days. I was still shaken by the whole situation with her and my brother.

I would've never thought this would have happened to them. In my eyes, they were the ideal couple, but even the picture-perfect couple had problems. Even though she did cheat on my brother, I still had love for her. Over the years she had been coming around, she had been the big sister I'd never had. I truly hoped that they both decided to work things out. While she and I talked on the phone, she gave me the impression that she was willing to work things out with my brother because she truly loved him. I just prayed that she and Jerome figured it all out.

Knock, Knock.

My nerves were through the roof at this point, when I heard the hard knocks at my door. I quickly ran to the front door and opened it to find my angel standing on the doorstep looking so beautiful. Tiffany and Jada ran toward the living room and embraced Faith in a big hug before they all ran toward the back to play with one another. I grabbed the pizza from the fridge and placed it on the table so I could get ready to heat it up. I had just placed the pizza in the oven when Trina finally decided to bring her ass in the house.

"When the pizza gone, we gone," she said with attitude.

I didn't even bother letting her nasty mood affect me. Instead, I couldn't help but eye her sexy ass. She was looking good as hell in her tight blue jeans with her hair pinned up, with some boots to match her tight black shirt. I turned my attention back toward the oven because staring at Trina had my dick getting hard. When the pizza was good and hot, I called the kids to come and eat. We all said grace and ate pizza while I told them about the three movies I had rented for them to watch. The kids were excited as hell and were trying to debate which movie they wanted to see first.

After everyone was done eating, we headed into the living room. I sat between Faith and Jada, and Tiffany was stretched out across the floor with her blanket, while Trina sat on the other side of the couch.

"It ain't going to happen." Trina snapped me back into reality.

I just smirked because she must have read my mind. Just having her under the same roof with me had me craving for her. I continued to watch the Peanut movie with the kids and decided it was best to keep my hands to myself. When the movie ended and the last slice of pizza was gone, Trina grabbed Faith and dipped out.

CHAMP

I really enjoyed the night with Trina and the kids, but unfortunately, Trina wasn't trying to get caught up with me. One thing I knew about Trina was that when she set her mind to something, she wasn't the type to change it for anyone. She was stubborn as hell when she made up her mind. Even though she didn't allow me to seduce her, she did finally open up about the Boston situation. She informed me that she was moving because of a job offer that she decided to take only because she felt it was going to help boost her career. The nigga who she claimed she was in love with had just opened up a law firm with his friend in Boston, and Trina decided it was best to go along and help them run the firm.

When Trina told me this, my heart started to hurt, but there was no way I was about to hinder her from doing something that she wanted to do. I sucked up my pride and decided to give her nothing but support and love. Before Trina left, she and I did come up with an arrangement for me to see Faith on a regular basis. As long as she was trying to better herself for our child, then there was no way I was going to hold her back.

I was pulled from my thoughts when I pulled up at Jada and Tiffany's grandmother's house.

"I enjoyed spending time with y'all," I told Jada and Tiffany as we talked to their grandmother's porch.

"We enjoyed you too," they said in unison.

"When y'all see y'all mother, give her a big hug for me."

They shook their head and gave me a big hug.

As we got closer to the front porch, Karen emerged from the house. The girls took off running to Karen and embraced her in a tight hug.

"Mommy, where Daddy?" Jada asked curiously.

Karen looked over at me, and we both looked at the kids.

Karen cleared her throat before bending down and telling them that their dad was out of town and was going to be home soon. The girls looked at one another and skipped into the house.

I was glad that neither of the girls understood what was going on between their parents; the less they knew the better for everyone.

I couldn't help but notice the scar on Karen's cheek. Damn, my brother didn't show her ass any mercy. Being angry and feeling betrayed made you do shit that you normally wouldn't do. Karen's face was still a little swollen, and she was still rocking two black eyes. She had always been a very beautiful woman, but I hated to see her this way.

Karen was about 160 pounds, pecan brown in complexion, with long jet-black hair.

"Karen, is everything good with you?" I asked.

"I'm good, Elijah. I mean, Champ," she said correcting herself.

She had been in the family long enough to know I wasn't a big fan of my first name.

"Did the girls give you any problems?" she asked as she stepped off the porch.

"No, I enjoyed them both. They kept me company."

"All them women you be smashing, I would have thought they would have gotten in your way," she joked playfully.

"Naw, these women around here be playing too many games. When it comes to my family, I drop everything."

"Yeah, these females around here do play games, but how Trina and Faith holding up?"

"Right about now, Trina trying to move to Boston. She got a job offer that she couldn't turn down."

"Damn, for real? Well, I know how you is about Faith, so I hope everything works out for y'all. Keep your head up."

I was trying to think about the pros of Trina leaving for this job, but I couldn't stop thinking about my baby being so far away from me."

"You still love her, don't you?"

"Who?"

"Trina," Karen said.

When Karen asked me that question, my heart felt as if it was about to fall out my chest. That was when I realized that I was still in love with Trina, and I wasn't over her like I thought. At this point in time, there was nothing that I could do about it. Changing her mind was probably a lost cause, but I wanted nothing more than to tell Trina how much I loved her and how much I needed her and Faith both in my life.

"Well, Champ, I'm about to let you go so I can enjoy the girls. I've missed my babies."

She gave me a hug before pulling away and asking me if I had heard anything from my brother. I could tell she was worried about him; I could hear it in her voice.

"Not today, but his lawyer told me that he was working on something."

I could see the disappointment on her face.

"I hate Jerome hit you like he did," I said as I unlocked my truck.

"It's okay," she muttered.

"It's never right to lay hands on a female. It doesn't matter if you were cheating on him or not."

She looked at me as if I had spoken a different language. She stepped closer to me before she told me what was on her mind.

"Look, Champ. I love your brother with all my heart and soul. I don't know what he told you…"

When I was about to speak, she immediately cut me off.

"I want you to know that I never cheated on him. Your brother has a lot of personal issues that he needs to deal with."

"Issues like what?" I asked with concern.

She shook her head at me.

"It's not my place to tell you. I'm going to let him tell you instead. I just pray that God removes that evil spirit out of Jerome."

She grabbed my hand and stared into my eyes. I saw the hurt and pain in them.

"I just want my husband back, Champ. If the man I met can't return, then I refuse to have anything to do with him. My girls and I deserve better than this."

I was completely lost because I had no idea what in the hell was going on. I was silently hoping that she was going to tell me, but she never did.

As soon as she released her hand from mine, I gave her a tender hug and told her goodbye. I hopped in the car and headed to the grocery store. As I drove through traffic, I couldn't stop thinking what was going on with Karen and my brother.

LATER THAT NIGHT

Knock, Knock.

I glanced over at my clock and noticed it was two in the damn morning. I groaned as I rubbed the sleep from my eyes. I had no clue who was knocking at the door, but I hurried to slide on my wife beater and headed toward the front door.

I wasn't expecting to see Trina standing there looking sexy as ever. She was holding a sleeping Faith in her arms.

"Trina, are you okay? Come in," I said with concern in my voice.

I hurried to cut on the living room light and stepped aside to let her pass.

I was thanking God in my head. Maybe Trina had finally changed her mind about leaving for Boston. I had been praying every day that God would change her mind about taking Faith away from me.

"Champ, I'm sorry for coming this late to your house," she began to apologize.

I took Faith from her arms and laid her sleeping body on my couch before giving Trina my full attention.

"No need to say sorry; you know you can come anytime you need to. Is everything okay?"

"No."

I bit down on my bottom lip as I waited for her to tell me what was going on with her.

"I know I told you that I wasn't going to leave until the first of the year. Well, I came to tell you that some things have changed. I'm going to be leaving in a few more hours."

"What!"

I felt as if a bullet had been shot through my heart. Tears stung my eyes because I wasn't anywhere near ready for Faith to leave.

"I'm sorry, Champ, but the company is up and running, and they need me ASAP. I just wanted to come over to let you know so you can tell Faith goodbye.

"Trina, I don't want you to leave, but I don't want you to stay and then miss a great opportunity. I just don't want to be the blame for that. So, go and handle your business."

"Thank you, Champ, for understanding," she said just before she kissed me on my lips.

When her lips met mine, I swear it felt as if the whole world had stopped. My heart began to race, and I wanted nothing more than to make love to her right then and there. Maybe she must have felt the same shit that I felt because Trina pulled away from me for only a moment before telling me to make love to her for the last time.

She grabbed me by the hand before leading me to the bedroom. As soon as we entered the room, I pushed her up against the wall before I started kissing and sucking on her neck. Her hands aggressively ripped open my wife beater just before she started kissing on my cheek. After we were both undressed, I took a step back as I eyed her sexy body. Her creamy skin and perfect figure were doing something to a nigga. My dick was on rock hard as I thought about all the things I wanted to do to her. Our tongues and lips played tag with one another's bodies. Her sweet moans sent chills throughout my body, and I was ready to give her the dick, but at the same time, I didn't want to rush things. I wanted this moment to last forever.

I pushed her down gently on the bed and slid between her thighs.

She moaned softly into my ear as I slid my rock-hard dick inside her tight pussy. Her juices were soaking a nigga up, and I was loving it.

"Just like that, baby," Trina kept crying in my ear.

The more she moaned and cried, the more I put pressure on her ass. I flipped her ass over on her stomach and slid back into her.

"Give it to me, Daddy!" Trina yelled out.

I thrust back and forth inside her as she gripped the bed sheets.

"Damn, Trina," I moaned as I began to dig deeper into her pussy.

Sweat was dripping from my face toward her back as I murdered her pussy.

"I'm about to cum," Trina cried out.

After Trina creamed on my dick, I caught me a fat as nut right behind her.

Within an hour, Trina was laying in my arms sound asleep. I brushed her hair out her face and watched her as she slept.

"I'm going to make you my wife one day," I muttered to her.

My eyes eventually grew heavy and sleep finally found me. I was tired as hell, but I was glad to have my queen sleeping right beside me.

I woke up a few hours later and lightly touched where Trina was sleeping at, but her side of the bed was empty. I sat up in bed and that's when I noticed that Trina was gone. I was just about go see if she was in the living room, but quickly changed my mind when I noticed a small note on her pillow. I picked up the note and began to read it slowly.

Champ, if you are reading this letter, then that means that you are finally aware that I'm gone. I didn't want to leave like this, but it was best for everyone. I couldn't face seeing Faith's face telling you goodbye. I want to let you know that you a great father to Faith. You mean the world to me, Champ, and you will always have a place in my heart. I love you so much. Please stay out of trouble."

Tears fell from my eyes as I reread the letter over three times before finally placing it back where I found it.

SASHA

A WEEK LATER….

I had no plans for today but to chill with Sweet Pea, but I really wasn't in the mood to chill with her either. I had so much going on in my life, and I wasn't interested in hearing Sweet Pea brag about the new nigga she was fucking and complaining about Rodney's trifling ass. She was my girl and all, but I just wanted to be left alone. Instead of going out, I decided to catch up on some household duties that I had started slacking off of.

I cleaned Malcolm's room first before I headed to Ashanti's room. It took me a little over an hour to clean the kids' room, and by then I was tired and exhausted, but I was on the move to get the house in tip top order again.

I had just stepped into the garage to grab some more trash bags to put in the trashcan when all the lights shut off. I began to panic because I was the only one who was supposed to be in the house, but apparently, someone else was with me. I tried cutting on the light in the garage, but nothing happened. My heart began to race as I started to slowly make my way back toward the door of the kitchen. As soon as I opened the door, I sniffed the air and I knew instantly someone was in the house or someone had just been here. I grabbed a butcher knife from the kitchen drawer as I tiptoed through the house. My heart was beating a mile a minute as I searched the house. Just when I thought the house was clear, that's when I noticed a dead rose on my pillow with a note.

I picked the note up with shaky hands as I began to read it aloud.

If you think you can get away from me, then you are one stupid bitch. I'm coming for you and the family you love if you don't give me what I want.

Tears fell down my face as I tore the letter up. I already knew who this letter was from. There was only one nigga who had it out for me, and that was Geno. Just when I thought his ass was dead and gone, he was back trying to ruin my life. I was filled with rage as I grabbed the dead rose and threw it and the letter in the trash. There was no way in hell I was about to let this nigga get me down. Even though I was saying all this shit, I knew deep down in inside I was scared as hell. This nigga knew where I stayed and probably knew everything it was about my family.

I wiped the tears from my eyes as I hurried to the laundry room. I had to get my mind off this shit. I had too much shit going on in my life to add Geno in the mix. I threw the clothes in the dryer and tried to calm myself down, but I was finding it hard to do.

When I picked up Ryan's pants to put them in the dryer, I heard change rattling in his pants, and I quickly began to empty his pockets. I silently cursed because Ryan never cleaned his pockets before throwing his shit in the dirty clothes.

When my phone began to blast Trey Songs' "Mind Fucking," my heart filled with joy again. All the anger and fear seemed to have evaporated into thin air. I already knew who it was even before I picked up the phone. Champ was the only nigga who had a special ringtone in my phone.

"How are you doing?" I asked.

I played in my hair as I waited for his response.

"I'm good, just trying to maintain. I'm missing Faith like hell. I can even hear her voice at night as I lay in bed," Champ said gently into the phone.

"I know it's hard, Champ, but if you need to talk or need company, you know I'm only a phone call away."

My heart ached whenever Champ was upset or hurting. I hated to see him this way, and I wanted nothing more than to cheer him up.

"I'm glad you decided to call me."

"You the only person I feel comfortable to vent to."

Just hearing him say that shit really put a smile on my face.

"What are your plans for today?" Champ asked.

"I'm just cleaning the house and doing laundry. What about you?"

"Nothing special. I'm just going to sit around the house and listen to music."

I guess Champ must have felt something was wrong with me because he quickly asked was I okay.

I wanted nothing more then to lie, but at the same time, I knew lying wouldn't get me anywhere.

"I'm not going to lie to you, I'm not okay. Matter of fact, I'm scared as hell right about now. He's back."

"Who's back?" Champ asked with confusion in his voice.

"Geno; he has found me again. He's back to make my life a living hell again," I muttered into the phone.

Champ didn't speak for the longest moment.

"Yeah, I know he's back," he finally admitted.

I was quiet as I waited on him to elaborate on what he meant.

I didn't want to tell you why I was locked up because I thought that I had handled the situation for you, but apparently, it ain't going to be handled until I put a bullet in his head. Geno is the nigga who walked up to me at the liquor store. He said some shit about you, and I didn't hesitate to beat the shit out of him. I thought I had almost killed his ass."

I held the phone tightly in my hands as I listened to Champ talk about his run-in with Geno. I remained silent as my mind began to race. What was I going to do? How was I going to get Geno to leave me the hell alone? Now that he had threatened to involve my family was what really had me on edge.

"Baby, are you okay?" Champ asked with concern in his voice.

"Yes," I managed to choke out.

"I know what you are thinking, but don't even think nothing crazy because I ain't going to let anything happen to you."

Just hearing Champ tell me he was going to protect me put my mind at ease. I still couldn't believe that Geno was the reason that Champ had gotten locked up. I was so engrossed in my feelings that I wasn't really paying attention to what I was doing until I started cleaning Ryan's pockets.

I was so ready to get off the topic of Geno. Talking about him only made me upset.

I picked the receipt that had fallen from Ryan's pocket and examined it to see where the receipt was from.

"Sasha, you there?"

"Yeah, I was just trying to see why this nigga got a hotel receipt in his pocket," I replied furiously.

"Damn, you for real?"

"Give me a minute. I will hit you back later," I told Champ before disconnecting our call.

I scrolled through my phone and hit Ryan's number. I got irritated when his phone sent me to voicemail. I stared down at the receipt and anger consumed me. I was at the point where I was ready to hop in my car and take a ride over to his job. But instead of going crazy, I quickly shot Champ a text letting him know that I was going to be over in a little bit after I got out the shower.

After I showered and got dressed, I stepped out the house with a brand-new attitude. I had that attitude of not giving a fuck. If he wanted to play games, I was down to play right along with him. Right before I could open my car door, I heard my name being called. I turned to the right, and that's when I spotted Tamera coming across the street.

"Sasha, I'm so glad that I caught you," she said, breathing hard as hell.

"What up with you?"

The bitch was looking crazy as hell and looked like she hadn't slept in days. Heavy bags were under her eyes, and she was rocking a nappy ass wig when she normally wore her real hair.

"Yeah, I've been making it. I was trying to catch Ryan before he left for work this morning."

Tamera reached into her purse and handed me some money.

"Tell him thanks for loaning me the money I needed."

I lifted my eyebrow at her and took the money from her, not really bothering to count how much she was giving Ryan back. I didn't show any emotion on my face, but my heart was racing with rage inside. How dare he give this bitch money without asking me first.

I watched as she ran back across the street, and that's when I hopped in the car and pulled out. I was sick to my stomach with the shit that Ryan was doing behind my back. Ryan had always been a sneaky ass, nigga and I had been with him for so many years that I knew when he was fucking, even though I didn't have any evidence against him.

I pulled up at Champs spot and decided to park alongside the road. I stepped out the car and adjusted my clothes just before I knocked on his front door. When our eyes met, my heart skipped a beat as I took his sexy ass in. He was looking fine as hell, and I wanted nothing more than to kiss his juicy lips. He pulled me aside and embraced me in a hug before our lips connected with one another. Just him pressed up against my body and our tongues dancing with one another had my pussy throbbing for his touch. When his lips left mine, I moaned into his ear. I was desperate for him to take me in his room and beat my pussy up, but I knew Champ was going to take his time with me like he always did.

I groaned when his lips began to caress the side of my neck and then my chest. He pulled away from me briefly as he removed his shirt as well as mine. He unsnapped my bra and flicked his tongue over my erect nipples. I cried out as he gently sucked on each nipple, caressing my pussy with his hand. He quickly unfastened my jeans before pulling them off me. I was standing there in my favorite lacy black Victoria's Secret matching bra and panty set. His eyes admired my naked body just before he began to caress me with his hand. He dropped to his knee and began to lick my pussy with his tongue. I could feel his tongue as he penetrated the fabric. I moaned when he pulled my panties down from my waist. He quickly picked me up and carried me to his leather couch where he slid between my legs.

I cried out as he put my legs over his shoulders and began to suck on my clit. Tears fell from my eyes as he made love to my pussy with his tongue. He licked and sucked on my clit until my legs began to shake, and I spilled my cream into his hungry mouth. I laid there in that position, not really trusting to move. Champ didn't show my pussy no mercy, and I was still having side effects from him eating me out. An hour later, Champ and I was stretched out on the floor chilling. I was drained to the point where I could barely feel my legs. Whenever I was stressing and just wanted to get away from it all, Champ always knew what to do and say to make me feel better. Champ had fucked me senseless, and I was still trying to recover. I moaned when Champ grabbed me and placed me on top of him. We were just about to get to round two when a knock came at Champ's door.

"Aye, Champ, this Dre. Open up."

Champ and I didn't speak we only stared at one another.

CHAMP

"Shit, you got to hide," I hissed at Sasha.

Sasha didn't move; instead, she looked at me like I was crazy.

"For what?" she asked with a frown on her face.

"Dre at the door."

She still sat there on the floor looking at me like what that had to do with her.

"Sasha, this is not the time."

I didn't want Dre to know that I was still fucking around with his sister when I had promised him that I was going to leave her alone. I quickly jumped up, grabbed Sasha's clothes off the floor, and threw them at her before pushing her toward the back part of the house. I hurried to put on my shirt and shorts.

"Sup, Bruh," I said as I opened the door.

"Shit, I just came over to check on you, Bruh," he said as he rubbed his hands together. "Are you good, Bruh? I mean, damn, your ass sweating like you a damn slave."

"Yeah, I'm good; just been working out," I lied.

"Bruh, you always working out. You can have all that shit; The only thing I'm going to be working out is pulling this trigger on these fuck niggas. But let me step inside right quick; I got to talk to you about some shit."

"Yeah, come on in."

My heart was racing and felt as if it was about to fall out of my chest. I was praying that Sasha knew how to shut the hell up and not say shit. I closed the door behind me as I followed Dre inside.

"Damn, bro. I know you ain't living like this. It's stinking like hell up in here," he said as he covered his shirt with his nose.

I chuckled before heading to the kitchen and pulling out a bottle of Glad. I sprayed the living room down to give it a fresh smell.

"Does that smell better?" I joked.

"Hell yeah, but anyway, I been doing some serious ass thinking about opening up this club."

I had a perplexed look on my face as I stared at him.

"I want you and me to run this club together. Since day one, you have been loyal to me. You the only person that I can trust with my life. Loyalty is everything to me. Even though I got mad with you about my sister, you ensured me that you were going to stop fucking with her, and so far, you have stood by your word. That means a lot." Dre kept on talking about how much he loved his sister, which only had my ass feeling guilty as fuck because Sasha and I had just gotten through fucking, and we were just about to fuck again before he pulled up. I felt bad as fuck that I had been lying to Dre about leaving his sister alone, but I didn't have the courage to tell him the truth. I just sat there and continued to listen to him as he preached about how loyal and real I was.

The whole time that he was talking, I could remember the words that my grandmother always told me when I was growing up.

"A woman can and will be a man's downfall if he allows it." And the statement rang so fucking true. I had no clue how I was going to get myself out of this situation. Even though Dre was my friend, I couldn't help that I had a thing for his sister. I couldn't help that the girl I was fucking with was his sister. Dre pulled his phone out and told me to hold on. He punched something into his phone, and that's when the craziest shit happened. A vibrating sound came from underneath my couch. We both looked at one another, but it was too late.

"Let me explain," I said as I watched Dre pick up Sasha's phone.

He stared back at me then bit down on his bottom lip before knocking me in the mouth. He didn't stop right there.

He kept hitting me with a few more blows. Somehow, he managed to get on top of me and threw two more punches, which I was able to dodge. Dre's face looked evil as hell, and I could tell he was furious. I used all my strength to flip his ass off me, but Dre wasn't going to stop fighting. He charged toward me, and that's when I hit his ass. I didn't want to hurt him because if I wanted to, Dre would have been laid out on the floor. Instead of Dre being relieved that I didn't murk his ass, he quickly kneed me in the nuts which brought me down to my knees.

"I should blow your fucking head off, nigga!" Dre yelled just before placing his pistol to my head.

"Do what you got to do, nigga."

I wasn't scared of death; my life was already fucked up.

"Shut up, nigga. Stop flexin'."

He gripped the pistol tighter as he hissed at me.

"This whole time you been lying to me about my sister, homie."

"I was going to tell you."

"Shut the fuck up! No you weren't!" Dre yelled before shoving the gun deeper into my head.

"Andre, stop!" Sasha screamed as she ran from the back.

When Dre pulled the gun away from my head, that's when I stood up and got back on my feet. Dre pointed his gun at me yet again and blasted me twice.

Pow, Pow!

SASHA

I held the pressure down on Champ's wound as blood leaked from his shoulder. My heart was beating a mile a minute as reality set in. My brother had just shot Champ. Tears fell from my eyes as I held on to Champ with all my strength. I was praying that he didn't die on me. Andre pushed me out the way and told me to go wait in the car. I didn't dare budge. There was no way I was about to leave Champ alone to die.

"Please, he needs a hospital," I cried.

"This shit burn like a bitch," Champ mumbled weakly.

"It's going to be okay, Champ," I managed to choke out.

I was relieved when Dre picked Champ up and carried him to the car. I was running right behind him. I hopped in the backseat and held Champ in my cars as Andre sped off towards the hospital. Blood spilled all over the seats as I held Champ in my arms. I still couldn't believe that Dre had shot Champ in the fucking shoulder. If Champ didn't live, there was no way that I could ever forgive my brother for taking the man I loved with all my heart away from me.

I could see the look of horror on Dre's face as he glanced toward Champ.

"We almost there, homie," Dre said emotionally.

We finally pulled up at the hospital a few moments later. Dre pulled up at the emergency side, hopped out the car, and ran inside to get someone to come help. A few seconds later, three nurses ran outside to get Champ and take him inside the hospital. Right before I was about to enter the hospital with Champ, Dre stepped in my way. I wasn't in the mood to fight with Dre; instead, I tried pushing past his ass so I could make sure that Champ was going to be okay. When Dre wouldn't let me pass, I began to get angry.

"Andre, you have done enough damage. Get the fuck out my way so I can go make sure Champ is okay."

Dre snatched me back and looked in my eyes.

"Sasha, look what time it is. You got to go pick up the kids from school. I will stay here and let you know how things go."

Just knowing Champ was going to be alone made me want to fight for him harder, but my hands were tied. I was first a mother before anything, and the kids was going to be waiting on me to pick them up from school very soon. I knew what Dre was telling me was true, and I didn't bother by fighting with him. Instead, I bit down on my bottom lip and grabbed Dre's keys that he had dangling in my face. I grabbed his keys and headed out the hospital. There was no way I could go and pick up the kids in bloody clothes, so I decided it would be best to head back home and change. The whole ride home, I was thinking about Champ and what had just gone down. I prayed that everything was okay with him.

I tried calling Sweet Pea, but she didn't answer. I had no one I could call on for help except only one person I didn't like, but I had no one else in my corner that I could depend on at the moment.

"Tamara, where you at?"

"On my way to the school house to pick up my kids."

"That's what's up. Can you do me a favor and pick up Malcolm and Ashanti for me?"

"Okay, no problem."

I was relieved when I found out I didn't have to pick up the kids. I was focused on getting my ass home so I could change and get my damn mind right before the kids stepped through the door. My whole body was shaking so bad that I could barely drive. It was with the help of the good Lord that I had even made it back home safely.

When I pulled up at my crib, I was relieved when I noticed that Ryan wasn't home. I cut the engine off and headed inside my crib. I quickly headed toward the shower so I could bathe all the blood from my skin. I stood in the shower it seemed forever, only to let the hot water caress my worn-down body. I also was talking to the man above and was asking him to forgive me for all the wrong that I had been doing. I knew what I had been doing was wrong as hell, but there wasn't a switch that I could press that could turn off what I was feeling. The love I had for Champ was stronger than ever and very much real. There was no way in hell that I wanted to give that up. When I stepped out the shower, I wasn't expecting to see Ryan sitting on the bed. All the madness came back to my mind of what I had seen when I was washing his clothes.

"Hey, baby," he said as he got off the bed and walked toward me.

"Don't 'hey, baby' me." I scowled as I walked past him and pushed his ass out my way.

"What's wrong with you?"

"You is what's wrong with me, Ryan. You walking around this bitch like you don't know what the fuck is going on."

"What are you talking about?"

I walked over to my purse and pulled out the hotel receipt. His whole face dropped to the floor when he noticed what I was holding in my hand.

"I see you ain't got shit to say now. You up here fucking around and actually thought that you wasn't going to get caught," I said vehemently as I pushed my finger against his forehead.

I was fed up with Ryan's shit. All he ever did was work; at least that was what he claimed he was doing. I knew in my heart that this nigga wasn't working as much as he claimed. I already felt in my heart this nigga was fucking up, but I had no proof. So when I found the receipt, I knew that my feelings were on point.

I left Ryan's ass in the middle of the floor, standing there looking confused. Even though Ryan was a good provider, there was still no way I was about to let him get away with fucking off on me. Even though I had been doing my own dirt, it was all because Ryan was out doing what the fuck he wanted. I never expected to fall in love with another man, but there was nothing that I could do to make this shit right.

I already knew the bitch he was probably fucking around with, and I was ready to beat the hoe down when she walked through the door with my damn kids. When a loud knock came at the door, I hurried to opened that bitch, and there stood Malcolm and Ashanti. They bum-rushed me with hugs and kisses, but I quickly peeled them off me and headed in Tamara's direction. I didn't hesitate to smack off the smirk that she was rocking on her face.

Wack!

She jerked back and held her face in shock.

I was waiting for the bitch to buck back so I could lay her ass out right there.

"Bitch, do me a favor and stay the fuck away from my husband!" I screamed at her.

I looked back toward Malcolm and Ashanti and noticed the shocked expression over their tiny faces. They had never seen me ever get out of character like this, so I could understand why they looked worried. I hated that my kids had to see me this way, but it was nothing that I could do to prevent the shit from happening like it had.

"Bitch, your ass is crazy!" Tamara yelled at me before running out my house.

I slammed the door behind her bitch ass and headed back upstairs with pure destruction in my mind. When I entered the bedroom, I noticed Ryan was on the bed going through his phone. I figured he had heard the commotion downstairs but wasn't in the mood to come down and suffer the same fate that I had just given one of his dumb hoes for fucking with him.

I didn't hesitate to snatch his phone from his hand so I could get his attention.

"Yo' ass just don't get tired, do you?" I asked furiously before throwing his phone against the wall.

"What the fuck is your problem, Sasha?" Ryan asked aggressively.

"Your cheating ass is the problem. I hope you know I just slapped that hoe you been fucking with behind my back."

"What bitch you slapped? I already told you I don't have no other bitches or hoes."

"Nigga, don't sit here and lie to me to my face. I know you been fucking 'round with Tamara. Out of all the bitches you could fuck, why that nasty bitch!" I screamed.

"Sasha, your ass is tripping. I ain't fucking that bitch. You need to get some rest because right now, you acting crazy as fuck," he said as he grabbed the door handle to leave.

This nigga just didn't understand how fucking mad he was making me. He was taking this like I was joking around with his ass, but I was being serious as hell.

There was no way I was about to let this nigga walk away from me. Oh, hell naw. It wasn't about to go down like that.

I hurried and pushed his ass out the way before slamming the door shut.

"Your ass ain't going no damn where. We going to talk about this shit."

"There ain't nothing to talk about, Sasha."

"What about the fact that you gave that bitch some fucking money? I want to know what the fuck is really going on."

Ryan didn't speak and couldn't even look me in the eyes.

"Yeah, you thought I wasn't going to find about the shit, didn't you?" I pushed his ass and waited for him to respond.

"Yeah, I gave her some money, but I didn't know—"

I cut that nigga off really quick with a slap across his face.

I knew if he had given her some fucking money that they had to be fucking on the low also. Just the thought of him fucking that nasty hoe in my damn bed was what had me wanting to murk his ass right where he stood. I couldn't control my anger and didn't hesitate to swing on his ass. I swung at his neck, his face, and anywhere else that I could reach. He finally grabbed my hand and shoved me up against the wall. My back hit the wall with a bang. He shouldn't have done that shit because I was ready to fuck his ass up. I rushed toward him and hit him on the chest as the tears fell from my eyes. Every emotion that I had been holding in finally rushed from my eyes as I cried out all my frustration.

I pulled away from him before I told his ass I that I wanted him out the house.

"Where am I supposed to damn go, Sasha?"

"You can go to hell for all I damn care."

CHAMP

It had been over a week since I had gotten shot, and I was still in pain. I was still hurting like hell and was still hurt about how the shit had all went down. Even though Sasha was having problems with her husband, she still found time to come by every day. When Dre came by and asked for forgiveness, I was speechless at first. I mean, should I forgive this nigga for shooting me? I didn't say shit to his ass at first, but he was persistent and came by every day to make sure a nigga was good. Even though I wanted to shoot his ass for even pointing a gun at me and shooting me, I figured to let the shit go and try to move on with my life. It was time that I put myself in his shoes, and that's when I realized that I had fucked shit up by fucking around with his sister. Dre and I were big on loyalty, but he felt I had betrayed his ass by messing with his sister when he told me not to.

After a few days of being laid up in the hospital, he and I came to a mutual agreement. Dre finally realized that his sister was grown as hell and had a mind of her own. I had been feeling Sasha a lot because she was different from the females I normally fucked around with.

Knock, Knock.

I slid off my couch and headed to the door. I swung it opened, and a smile crossed my face when I noticed Sasha standing there looking sexy as hell. Her perfume tickled my nose as she smiled at me. She had no clue how happy I was to see her sexy ass. I was getting used to getting her wonderful massages that she came to give me once I had come home.

"Damn, you must be happy to see me," she said, giving me that brilliant smile.

"You know I am," I mumbled before giving her a kiss.

"Well you ain't the only one. I'm happy to see you as well. How your shoulder holding up?" Sasha asked before she threw her purse on the couch and began rubbing the top of my shoulder with her hand.

"It still kind of hurts when I move it, but overall, I'm okay. I just want all this shit to be over with."

"Well, it will all be over in a couple more weeks. I stopped by the pharmacy to pick up your other prescription the doctor gave you for the pain."

"I hate taking pills, but these bitches take all the pain away and put a nigga to sleep." I chuckled.

"Well, I don't want your ass in pain, so you better take your medicine, but you know something, Champ…"

She had my full attention as I waited for her to finish her sentence.

"I really enjoy being around you, and my feelings for you are real strong. Late at night while I'm lying in bed, I be wishing you was there with me."

She grabbed my hand before staring into my eyes.

"Am I wrong for that?"

I was speechless. Sasha was opening all the way up to me. I could feel every word she was saying, and she had me in my feelings.

"Sasha, I can't even lie. I feel the same way about you too. I sit around and think about you all the time when you're not around. You asked me was you wrong for feeling like that, and all I can say is follow your heart. At the end of the day, you should do what feels right for you. I can tell you all day to leave your husband, but that isn't my decision. I just don't see myself telling you to leave your husband to be my lady. I'm going to always love you whether you my lady or not, but if you want to be with a nigga, then you got to be ready to take it to the next step."

I watched her as the tears began to fall from her eyes.

"Champ, you right, I can't lie. I love Ryan to death, but I'm not happy with him anymore," she confessed as she wiped the tears from her face.

"It going to be okay," I ensured her. "Since you been looking out for me, I'm do something for you."

"Like what?"

"What did you eat today?"

"Nothing really, why?"

"Well, I'm about to cook for you."

She smiled at me, because I guess she was shocked that I knew how to cook and was willing to cook a nice hot meal to make her feel better.

I headed to the kitchen and opened the cabinets and refrigerator as I grabbed everything I needed to fix the meal. Sasha came to the small island, pulled up a bar stool, and watched as I worked my way around the kitchen. I was about to make her the best salad that she had ever tasted. I took out the carrots, onions, red peppers, virgin olive oil, a small thing of pulled chicken, lettuce, and white cedar. I took out a large pan and poured a small amount of olive oil in the pan before I added the chicken and vegetables.

After I was done making up the salad, I fixed her a plate and poured her a glass of red wine. I could see the desire on her face as she dug into her salad.

"Mmm, this shit is so delicious," she said with excitement in her voice.

"Thank you. I'm glad you like it."

I grabbed her fork out her small hands and started to feed her the rest of her salad. Every time I stuck the fork in her mouth, our eyes connected as if we were one. I didn't know what it was about Sasha, but she had a nigga all the way open. After she took her last bite, she licked her lips before sliding her tongue in my mouth. Our tongues danced with one another as she rubbed her hand up and down my dick print.

I groaned when she unzipped my pants.

"Shit!" I moaned as she wrapped her lips around my dick and began to suck me off. I pulled her hair to the side as she stared into my eyes. I couldn't help but moan her name when she began to slurp on my dick. The shit she was doing was driving me crazy as hell. She pulled my dick out her mouth, spit on it, and sucked it back into her mouth like she was a porn star. I closed my eyes as I rubbed my hands through her mangled hair.

"Champ, this dick so damn good. I love this dick," Sasha confessed.

"I love you too," I heard myself saying.

I was so caught up in the moment that I had slipped around and told her I loved her. She increased her speed with her mouth after I had said those three words. I gripped her hair with a cobra grip as I endured the loving that she was throwing on a nigga.

"Cum for me daddy," she commanded.

There was no point of me holding back on her, and a few moments later, I released my seeds into her mouth.

"You taste so damn good," she said as she licked her lips clean.

I felt drained as hell, and I guess Sasha must have known this, because she gladly zipped my pants back up just before placing a kiss on my lips.

"Well, baby, I got to go."

"Okay," I mumbled.

Damn. After she had sucked my soul from me, I was hoping she was going to stay around and chill with a nigga. Even though I was disappointed, I didn't dare show it on my face.

"I really enjoyed the lunch you prepared for me."

She grabbed her purse off the couch before turning back toward me.

"You really surprised me with your cooking skills. Thank you, baby."

"I'm glad you enjoyed it. Be safe and be good."

"I promise to be good," she said before opening the door and stepping outside.

"Aye, Champ... Did you mean what you said earlier?"

"Mean what?"

"Did you mean that you love me back there?"

I licked my lips before staring at her.

"Yeah, I meant that shit."

"I love you too," she said before closing the door behind her.

SASHA

I couldn't believe that Champ told me he loved me. I felt like a million dollars as I drove down the road. Everything was happening so damn fast, but I was loving every moment of it. Champ had made valid points about being with him. I knew he told me it was all up to me to leave Ryan and be with him. It was a huge step to leave Ryan. He wasn't just my husband, but he was my kids' father. Whatever decision I made, I knew it was going to be a life changing one. If I stayed with Ryan, the chances of me being happy were very slim, but if I left him and got with Champ, I felt like I would be happy.

How would the kids respond to him? I thought to myself.

Champ told me to follow my heart, but I was still at a standstill because I had kids I had to take into consideration.

While I waited on the traffic light to change, I decided to make a right and head to the kids' school. I grabbed my phone and sent Ryan a text message, telling him to meet me at home that he and I needed to talk about something important.

He sent me a text message a few seconds later and told me that he was heading home. Ryan had been sleeping in a hotel not far from where we stayed due to me putting his ass out. Even though I got lonely at night, I never once called his ass to tell him to come back home. When I pulled up at the school curb, Malcolm and Ashanti were standing outside waiting on me. I knew the problems that Ryan and I were having was affecting the kids, because every night, Malcolm made sure to check on me to make sure that I was okay, but Ashanti had taken a different attitude toward me and had started acting sour about the fact I had put her dad out.

"How was y'all day?" I asked as they got in the car.

"It was good, Ma. I passed my math test today," Malcolm joyfully said as he showed me the enormous A on his test paper.

"That's good, baby. I'm so proud of you," I said as I brushed his hair back from his face.

"How was your day, Ashanti?"

"It was alright," she mumbled as she rolled her eyes. "When can I see my daddy? Why he ain't living with us anymore? Are ya'll going to get a divorce?" she asked with attitude in her voice.

"Ashanti!" Malcolm yelled before giving her a look that I had never noticed before.

"It's okay, Malcolm. Y'all need to hear this."

I turned down the music so they could hear my every word.

"Me and your father are going through some things right now, and at this point, I don't know what's going to happen with us. I love your father to death, but we just ain't seeing eye to eye right about now."

"So y'all going to get a divorce?" Ashanti asked emotionally.

Tears ran down her face, and it hurt me to my soul to see her this way. I knew that if I decided to leave Ryan, Ashanti was going to take it the hardest.

The more I tried explaining to her about Ryan and I, tears continued to pour down her face. Malcolm just stared at me before giving me an expression that told me that everything was going to be okay.

I pulled into my driveway a few moments later and parked right beside Ryan's car. Ashanti jumped out the car and ran toward the front door, while Malcolm slowly walked behind her.

The door swung open and Ryan greeted the kids.

I took a deep breath as I made my way into the house. My decision had been made. I only prayed that the decision I was making was the right one.

"Malcolm and Ashanti, go put your things up in your room. Let me and your mom talk for a little bit," Ryan told the kids as he stared at me.

"Okay, Daddy. I love you," Ashanti said before embracing her father in a hug.

The kids vanished into their rooms which only left Ryan and I standing there. My heart began to race because I had no clue where this conversation was going to leave us. Ryan stepped to me, and I closed my eyes for a split second as I got the courage that I needed to tell Ryan how I was truly feeling.

"Baby, I miss you so much," Ryan confessed as he grabbed my hand.

His touch was so warm, but it didn't move me like it once did.

"I love you so damn much, and I'm so sorry about everything that I done put you through," Ryan said emotionally.

"I can't lie, I miss you also," I confessed.

"Let me come back home and make this shit right," he said as he pulled me toward him, but I quickly pulled away.

"Ryan, I'm not going to lie to you, but I haven't been happy for a very long time."

"What do I need to do to make you happy, baby? Do you want a bigger house? I will give you anything you desire."

"You just don't get it, do you?"

His face went blank.

"What do you want, Sasha?"

"I want a divorce Ryan."

I didn't even give Ryan enough time to respond before I grabbed my keys and headed back to my car. I was just about to pull out the driveway when he began to beat his hand up against my car.

"Baby, please don't leave me. What about the kids?"

I didn't dare stop the car. Instead, I peeled out of the parking lot as quickly as I could. Seeing the tears in Ryan's eyes had torn me up inside. I wanted to get out of there as quickly as I could before I changed my mind. As I drove down the road, the voice in my head told me that I had just made the correct decision. I wanted to be loved, and in my heart, I knew that Ryan probably could never give me the type of love and attention that Champ did.

CHAMP

(THIRTY MINUTES EARLIER)

Knock. Knock.

As I headed to the door, I had a smirk on my face because I thought it was Sasha coming back for round two. I wanted her fine ass, but at the same time, I wasn't about to pressure her to do anything that she wasn't ready to do on her own. I wanted nothing more than to kiss her sexy lips as I opened my front door, but I was oddly shocked when I noticed Trina standing there on my steps.

"Trina, what you are doing here?" I asked with a confused look on my face.

"I had to come get the rest of my things from my mom's house. I didn't want to come to town and not see you, plus, I heard you had gotten shot, so I was worried about you.

I was surprised she had even gotten the news, but I should have known Trina wasn't going to dip out on a nigga and not know what was going on with me.

"Yeah, a nigga got shot, but it isn't nothing major though, so you ain't got to worry about me."

I stepped aside to let her fine ass in. I couldn't take my eyes off her. She was looking like she had just stepped out of a magazine shoot. She was rocking her business suit and was looking like she was about to sign a million-dollar deal.

"Which crazy hoe shot your ass?" she asked with a little attitude as she placed her hand on my shoulder.

I laughed at her ass before stepping away from her.

"It's good to see you, Trina. Where my baby at?"

"She at my mom's house."

I could tell how Trina was staring at me that she had some serious shit on her mind.

She licked her sexy lips, and I grew weak in the knees. She took a deep breath before she told me exactly what she was thinking in her mind.

"Come with me, Champ... back to Boston."

I looked up at her in utter shock. I wanted to make sure that I had actually heard her correctly.

"There is nothing here in Albany, Champ. When I heard that you had gotten shot, it hurt me to my soul. Just the thought of losing you scared the shit out of me. I thought that I was going to lose you to the streets again," she confessed emotionally as she walked closer to me.

Damn, a nigga couldn't even speak because this was not what I was expecting to hear come out of Trina's mouth. She and I had been through so much, but I never once thought that she and I could ever be with one another again. I took a deep breath trying to soak everything that Trina had just thrown on a nigga.

"Champ, I love you, and I need you back in my life."

She stared at me with those big beautiful eyes, and my heart began to race. I had been waiting to hear her say this shit since I got out of prison.

"We need you in our lives, Champ. Let's be a family like we always dreamed and talked about," she said gently as she rubbed the side of my face.

When she touched me all my doubts disappeared and she was all I saw.

"So, what you going to do?" she asked.

"I'm coming with you, baby."

When I said that shit, her lips touched mine.

We kissed so passionately it felt like the world had stopped. I wanted to take her at that very moment and make sweet love to her, but I knew her, and I didn't have time for all that right now. She looked around me and told me that I needed to put my stuff in storage and just pack what I needed as far as clothes, shoes, etcetera.

As I packed my shit up, I began to think of Sasha and what we could've had. Now that Trina had come into my life and told me that she wanted us to be a family, I couldn't deny her that shit because deep down inside, I always wanted that, but at the time, Trina didn't want a nigga back.

I wasn't about to pass up this opportunity to be with my family, when I knew that Sasha wasn't about to leave her husband or kids for me.

Knock, Knock.

Trina and I both looked at one another, but she continued to pack some of my things while I headed to the door to see who it was knocking.

I was in a good ass mood, but when I opened the door, all the joy fell from my chest. My heart was beating in overdrive when I noticed Sasha standing in front of me.

SASHA

"Sasha!"

"Aye, baby," I said as I tried to hug Champ.

He stepped outside the door and closed it behind him.

"Sasha, we need to talk."

"Yeah, I got some good news for you, baby."

"Let me tell you first, Sasha. I care about you a whole lot. You are a wonderful person to be around, and you different from any other female that I have ever came in contact with, but I think you need to know that Trina just came back, and she and I decided to work things out. I just want to tell you that I'm sorry if I misled you."

His words cut through my heart like a knife.

"I'm leaving Albany to go stay in Boston."

"That's good for you, Champ, and I hope y'all be happy," I managed to choke out before I walked off from him.

I was hurt because I had just abandoned my damn family to be with this man.

"Sasha, what did you have to tell me?"

"It wasn't important."

I gave him a half smile before getting back in my car and pulling out his complex. I felt like a damn fool for even telling Ryan I wanted to leave him to be with Champ. I swerved in and out of traffic, praying that Ryan was still home and hadn't left yet. I was speeding through traffic like a crazy woman. I was grateful that no police were in sight, because I would have gotten pulled over and given a damn ticket for reckless driving.

I pulled up at my driveway a few moments later and was relieved to see Ryan's car was still parked in the same spot. I threw my car in park and hurried into my house. The house was quiet as hell, which I found strange. I called out Ryan's name, but I got no answer from him. I headed to my room, and that's when my whole world came crashing down on me.

Tears fell from my eyes when I saw blood coming from Malcolm, Ashanti, and Ryan's bodies. I lost my balance and fell to the floor as the tears fell down my cheeks. I screamed and yelled as I cried for my family. I crawled toward the bed, and that's when I noticed a small note that was written by Ryan.

Sasha, I couldn't take it not having you in my life. I love you with all my heart and soul. I never wanted to hurt you. I tried to make you happy, and knowing that I never accomplished that hurt me to my soul. I never wanted to hurt you. All I ever wanted to do was love you. I'm sorry for taking the kids from you, but there was no way they were going to be able to cope with your decision. Good bye.

I fell straight to the floor and everything went dark.

A WEEK LATER

THE FUNERAL

I wasn't the same, and I highly doubted that I ever would be. Losing my family was the worst feeling in the world. I hadn't been able to sleep or eat since coming home to my whole family dead. I still couldn't believe that Ryan had taken the kids with him. Why did he have to kill the kids too? I kept crying out and asking myself. I hated myself. I had fucked around and gambled on my family and had made a bad choice by leaving my family that day to go chase a man who didn't give a fuck about my ass. Hot tears fell from my eyes, and I brushed them away.

I didn't even want to go to the funeral, but I made my way in the church so I could say my last goodbyes to my family. As I headed inside the church, I noticed it was filled up to the rim and there weren't any pews left. Teachers, kids, coworkers, and family members had the church on lock. I walked slowly to the front with Dre walking beside me. If it hadn't been for him, I highly doubt I would have made it to the funeral in the first place. This shit was the most painful thing that I had to go through. I sat on the first row and tears fell from my eyes as I stared at the pictures of my kids. I felt many hands touching and rubbing on my back as they tried to comfort me, but it was no amount of words that could take the hurt away. This wasn't something that I was ever going to live and get over. My whole family was gone from one wrong move.

My brother Dre held me tightly as I cried my eyes out.

"It's going to be okay, Sasha. I got you, sis," Dre whispered in my ear.

I leaned on my little brother as the service carried on.

The funeral was sad as hell. For a moment, I felt as if I was going to pass out, but I was grateful that I didn't. When the service was over, I didn't dare move. My brother had tears in his eyes and took it upon himself to accept all condolences for me. He held me briefly and kissed me on my forehead before he left me to talk with some of the family members that wanted to show their condolences to me.

"Excuse me."

I looked up at the person who had just spoken, not really knowing who she was. I had never seen her before. The woman was dark skinned and was very pretty.

"My name is Trina Anderson." When she spoke her name, anger filled my soul. This was the bitch who was at one point in time blowing up Ryan's phone. I always had suspicions that he was fucking this bitch because they spent a little too much damn time for my liking. She seemed to look familiar, and as I looked at her, I noticed that I had seen her picture in Champ's apartment a while ago.

"How dare you show your fucking face here," I spat at the bitch.

The woman ignored my outburst and began to introduce herself.

"You don't know me, but your husband was a good man. He was like a mentor to me. He taught me everything I needed to know to become the lawyer that I am today. I just came to show my respects."

I swear I wasn't in the mood at the moment, and I was beyond fired up.

I stood up and stared at her.

I didn't want to hear shit about that cheating ass nigga. He killed my damn babies!

"Sasha, Ryan wasn't cheating on you; you were his heart and soul. I don't know why he did what he did, but I know for a fact he never cheated on you."

"How can you explain all them hotel receipts that I found in his pockets?"

"I have someone that can explain that to you," she said just before she signaled for someone to come over to where we were standing up at.

When I looked up and noticed Champ, anger consumed me. I blamed his ass for why I was really here in the first place. Champ was the last nigga that I ever wanted to damn see. If I would have never met him and fell in love, my family would still have been here today. Now I wished I would have listened to my brother when he warned me to leave his homie alone. I had been so stubborn thinking that I knew everything, and now I had lost everything that I cared about. Now as I looked at my babies in the casket, I realized none of that shit was worth it.

I couldn't even believe that he even had the nerve to show up at the funeral.

"What are you doing here, Champ?" I asked with anger in my voice.

"Hold up, y'all already know one another?" Trina asked us both.

"Yes, I know him. He is friends with my brother Andre," I muttered as I stared into Champ's eyes.

"There was no way I was about to not come for support," Champ said softly.

Tears fell from my eyes.

"I don't want your ass here," I spat at him.

I was so emotional that I didn't even notice that the bitch Trina Anderson was still there.

"Champ, I will be in the car," Trina said to Champ.

Champ nodded before his eyes met mine again.

"That's your bitch?" I asked tearfully.

He nodded.

"That's my baby mama," he mumbled.

"Your baby mama was working with my husband," I said gently.

Champ didn't speak at first; instead, he cleared his throat and kept staring at me.

"Sasha, I'm so sorry for your loss, but when I found out that Ryan was your husband, it took me by surprise. Ryan wasn't cheating on you; at least not with a female."

I wiped the last of my tears before I stared into his eyes.

"What the fuck you mean he wasn't cheating on me, at least not with a female? You making it seem that he was still cheating just not with a bitch. Don't come here playing games with me, Champ," I said viciously.

Champ cleared his throat before he looked around to make sure no one wasn't in ear shot.

"When your husband killed himself, I found out from my brother that he knew him very well. Apparently, they were best friends/lovers." I felt as if I was going to be sick to my stomach.

"Ryan wasn't gay," I managed to choke out.

Champ didn't speak at first, but when I glanced up at him, I knew he wasn't lying. He was saying nothing but the truth.

"The hotel receipts that you found in Ryan's pockets that time, turned out to be the receipts from a time when Ryan and my brother Jerome would go meet one another. At first Jerome told me that Ryan took him under his wing and tried his best to get him off drugs and keep him out the streets. Then one thing led to another, and that's when a relationship started to develop. You were right all along, Sasha. You told me plenty of times that you thought Ryan was creeping, but you never had proof. Well, you weren't crazy, but he wasn't creeping with who you thought it was."

I stared at Champ, but the words that were at the tip of my tongue couldn't leave my mouth. Tears fell down my cheeks because all of this could have been prevented if I would have tried to communicate with my husband better. I was angry and disgusted that I had no clue that my husband was fucking another man behind my back.

My heart was broken, and I felt so empty inside that I was burying my whole fucking family, and the man whom I had been married to, I knew nothing about him or his secret life he was living. I couldn't accept what I was just told and ran straight out the church.

I had to get the hell out of there. My life was so fucked up. I had cheated on my husband with a man who didn't love me and who had just gotten back with his baby mama. My husband had been gay the whole time and I had no damn clue that he was. I had lost my whole fucking family, and now I was going to spend the rest of my days alone. I couldn't bear it. It was no way I was going to be able to survive this situation.

I tried my best to find the nearest vehicle, but the tears were blinding my vision. I spotted a woman stepping out her car and ran toward her. I pushed her out the way before jumping in her car and throwing the car into gear. I sped off, not really knowing where I was going. The blaring the horns was all I heard before I ran a red light and ran straight into an 18-wheeler. There was no way I was going to be able to live knowing that I was the reason my whole family was dead. When everything went dark, I didn't fight it; instead, I embraced it.

EPILOGUE

CHAMP

2 YEARS LATER

Knock, Knock.

My face immediately turned into a smile when I glanced out the peephole. I had been waiting on this news for the last year when this plan was first sat into effect.

"What's up, Bruh?" I said as I opened the door.

"Everything done," Dre said as he took off his black gloves.

I didn't say anything; just nodded my head to the sound of his voice.

"Damn, I wish I could have been with you, Bruh," I muttered as I tried to picture Geno's facial expression when Dre ran down on him.

After Sasha killed herself, Dre and I had stopped fucking around with one another. He blamed me for his sister killing himself, and I sort of blamed myself also. I could barely eat or sleep after I heard the tragic news. I still found myself crying about how the shit went down, but there was nothing that I could do to make the shit go away or go back to change how things went down.

Dre and I had gone a whole year without speaking, until one day he pulled up at my crib, and we sat down and had a long ass talk about his sister. It was finally time for us to forgive one another and move on. Sasha wouldn't have wanted us to be beefing over her, but I understood the pain that Dre was feeling because I was feeling the same amount of pain.

After Dre and I finally got back cool, he and I both decided to find Geno and put his ass to sleep for all the shit that he had put Sasha through when she was living. I guess we wanted to get rid of Geno because I knew for a fact that if he was dead, Sasha was going to rest peacefully knowing he was in hell burning for the rest of eternity.

I guess when Sasha found out the truth, that was what sent her over the edge. Even though Dre and I had set our differences aside, I still felt as if I was partially to blame why she was no longer here on this Earth. I wanted to make shit right, and the only way I felt that would happen was if I got rid of Geno.

"Naw, Bruh. My conscious wouldn't let me get down like that. Killing Geno was only for me to do. You already know Trina would fuck a nigga up if she even thought I was trying to get you back to the street life."

We both looked at one another and started laughing.

I shook my head at Dre's comment because he wasn't lying. Since I put that ring on Trina's finger, she was taking her role as my wife serious as hell, but I wasn't complaining. My life was great, and I was happy as hell to finally have my family back with me.

Dre and I had just opened up a club together when I decided to get my fitness gym going. I wanted a change of career, and Dre finally wore a nigga down about helping him run his club that he wanted to one day open. Now that it was open and running, I wasn't going to lie; I was making more money than I had ever made before. Going into business with my partna was the best decision that I had ever made. To give honor to his sister, Dre and I decided to name the club Sasha. Even though Sasha was no longer here, I still felt like her spirit was somewhere nearby. I just prayed that she was resting peacefully.

THE END

TO MY READERS,

I really hope that you enjoyed What He Don't Know Won't Hurt/ A Lustful Love Triangle story. I put my blood, sweat, and tears into bringing a good novel to you. I have many more coming on the way. Thank you for supporting me. Remember, love is like a powerful drug. Please don't misuse it.

Love,

Author Nikalos

ABOUT THE AUTHOR

What He Don't Know Won't Hurt

Nikalos was born in Georgia. His mother is his greatest inspiration and always encourages him to be the best writer that he can be. He fell in love with reading and writing romance at an early age but never dreamed that he was going to be an author. Right now, Nikalos is the author of What He Don't Know Won't Hurt and Thoughts of A Savages. His dream is to be the best writer that he can be and entertain each and every one of his readers.

Connect with Nikalos On Social Media:

Facebook Personal Page: Author King Nikalos

Facebook Author Page: Author King Nikalos

Instagram: KingNikalos

ACKNOWLEDGEMENTS

First off, I want to give all praise to the highest God for making all this possible. God is the only way. To my beautiful mother that I love so much, thank you for not giving up on me. To Ms. Ebony Bryant, thank you for everything; you have been a blessing to my life, thank you :-) To my brothers, Mike and Chris, yo' lil bro luv you! Everything is going to be okay. I promise I got us! To my lil' cousins, Yasmen, Tye, EJ, JT, Big Man, Dee, Big Ma, Boo, Freddy, and the rest of Pam's kids, I love y'all so much. I want y'all to be great! Zykiah, thank you for being a good friend. To my Favorite LIL' BIG CUZ, Lovetta Brown, I miss you. I'm proud of you, too. To all my nieces and nephews, I love you y'all. To Neil Lewis, Yokubi (N.O), Shawty Lo, Hellboi, Marquette, Jabo, Snoop, 229 crew, Quiet, Slim, and everyone that gave me any type of inspiration; Eric T, Money, Vess Tyson, Tra William, Harry Jackson, Big G, Monique, Tameka,Auntie, A.Ford, Meat, Ohio , Cocoa □, Walt, Farley, Dirty D, the whole F2; Sapp, I appreciate you, bruh, for helping me with my law work. You came through for da kid!

Special thanks to My wonderful Editor Nerrisa Keep grinding you bring every time. One Love

To Solakin Publication, thank you for giving me a chance to broadcast my talent.

To my grandma, Mrs. Jewell, I miss you every single day. I know you up in the sky looking down. I love you ... The SKY IS THE LIMIT ....

Send manuscript to solakinpublication@gmail.com

FOLLOW US FACEBOOK

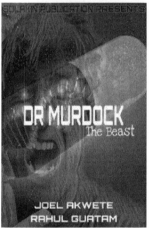

SOLAKIN PUBLICATIONS BOOKS

COMING SOON!!

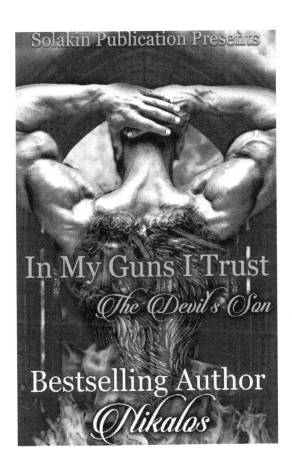

What He Don't Know Won't Hurt

Made in the USA
Columbia, SC
24 April 2023